# THE MAGNIFICENT MARQUIS

The Marquis drove for about three miles away from Lord Durham's house.

Then he turned off the road into a small wood and up a rough track running between the trees.

He pulled the horses to a standstill as they could go no further.

He fixed his reins, climbed out and walked round to the back of his chaise.

The fragment of blue ribbon he had noticed on his departure was still hanging out of the box that was there to hold luggage or extra rugs for cold weather.

He pulled open the door and said quietly,

"You can come out now."

A small frightened face looked up at him.

He recognised that it was the face of someone very young yet exceedingly beautiful.

She stared at him.

Then she asked in a soft childlike voice,

"How – did you know – I was here?"

"Before I got into the driving seat, I saw a piece of your sash sticking out."

There was no reply.

# THE BARBARA CARTLAND PINK COLLECTION

## Titles in this series

# THE MAGNIFICENT MARQUIS

# BARBARA CARTLAND

Barbaracartland.com Ltd

# THE BARBARA CARTLAND PINK COLLECTION

Barbara Cartland was the most prolific bestselling author in the history of the world. She was frequently in the Guinness Book of Records for writing more books in a year than any other living author. In fact her most amazing literary feat was when her publishers asked for more Barbara Cartland romances, she doubled her output from 10 books a year to over 20 books a year, when she was 77.

She went on writing continuously at this rate for 20 years and wrote her last book at the age of 97, thus completing 400 books between the ages of 77 and 97.

Her publishers finally could not keep up with this phenomenal output, so at her death she left 160 unpublished manuscripts, something again that no other author has ever achieved.

Now the exciting news is that these 160 original unpublished Barbara Cartland books are already being published and by Barbaracartland.com exclusively on the internet, as the international web is the best possible way of reaching so many Barbara Cartland readers around the world.

The 160 books are published monthly and will be numbered in sequence.

The series is called the Pink Collection as a tribute to Barbara Cartland whose favourite colour was pink and it became very much her trademark over the years.

The Barbara Cartland Pink Collection is published only on the internet. Log on to www.barbaracartland.com to find out how you can purchase the books monthly as they are published, and take out a subscription that will ensure that all subsequent editions are delivered to you by mail order to your home.

## NEW

Barbaracartland.com is proud to announce the publication of ten new Audio Books for the first time as CDs. They are favourite Barbara Cartland stories read by well-known actors and actresses and each story extends to 4 or 5 CDs. The Audio Books are as follows:

| | |
|---|---|
| The Patient Bridegroom | The Passion and the Flower |
| A Challenge of Hearts | Little White Doves of Love |
| A Train to Love | The Prince and the Pekinese |
| The Unbroken Dream | A King in Love |
| The Cruel Count | A Sign of Love |

More Audio Books will be published in the future and the above titles can be purchased by logging on to the website www.barbaracartland.com or please write to the address below.

If you do not have access to a computer, you can write for information about the Barbara Cartland Pink Collection and the Barbara Cartland Audio Books to the following address:

Barbara Cartland.com Ltd., Camfield Place,
Hatfield, Hertfordshire AL9 6JE, United Kingdom.
Telephone: +44 (0)1707 642629
Fax: +44 (0)1707 663041

# THE LATE DAME BARBARA CARTLAND

Barbara Cartland who sadly died in May 2000 at the age of nearly 99 was the world's most famous romantic novelist who wrote 723 books in her lifetime with worldwide sales of over 1 billion copies and her books were translated into 36 different languages.

As well as romantic novels, she wrote historical biographies, 6 autobiographies, theatrical plays, books of advice on life, love, vitamins and cookery. She also found time to be a political speaker and television and radio personality.

She wrote her first book at the age of 21 and this was called *Jigsaw*. It became an immediate bestseller and sold 100,000 copies in hardback and was translated into 6 different languages. She wrote continuously throughout her life, writing bestsellers for an astonishing 76 years. Her books have always been immensely popular in the United States, where in 1976 her current books were at numbers 1 & 2 in the B. Dalton bestsellers list, a feat never achieved before or since by any author.

Barbara Cartland became a legend in her own lifetime and will be best remembered for her wonderful romantic novels, so loved by her millions of readers throughout the world.

Her books will always be treasured for their moral message, her pure and innocent heroines, her good looking and dashing heroes and above all her belief that the power of love is more important than anything else in everyone's life.

*"Happiness is in the mind. When you are tired, ill or miserable, try making a picture of beauty and tell yourself a story of love. If you do it frequently you will find yourself both happier and lovelier in body and soul."*

Barbara Cartland

# CHAPTER ONE
# 1868

The Marquis yawned and sighed,

"I must get up now."

The woman lying beside him moved a little closer.

"Don't go yet, darling Rex," she murmured. "It is so marvellous and exciting when you love me."

"It is indeed," replied the Marquis, "but I have an engagement for early tomorrow morning and I must catch a little sleep."

A soft arm wound round his neck.

"I heard just today," she whispered, "that George is worse – and the doctors do not think he will live very much longer."

There was a little pause before she carried on,

"Then maybe, darling, we can be together *for ever*. It will be the most wonderful thing that has ever happened to me."

It was with the greatest difficulty that the Marquis did not stiffen.

He merely responded,

"Take care of yourself and do not do too much."

Despite the soft hands holding him back he climbed out of bed.

He dressed himself quickly with the expertise of a gentleman who could manage without a valet.

Then he walked towards the bed.

The dark-haired and alluring beauty, with whom he had spent so much time these past weeks, was waiting for him.

She held out her arms, but he just took one of her hands in his.

"Thank you, Silvia, for a memorable evening."

His lips touched her skin and then he turned to the door.

She gave a little cry.

"Rex! Rex! Please kiss me again."

He pulled the door open and looked back.

"I have to leave you, go to sleep, Silvia, and dream of me."

"You know I will do that," she pouted.

He ran down the stairs, pulled open the front door and let himself out.

He only had a short way to walk to his own house and he set off at a quick pace.

He was aware that he was running away from yet another trap – and there had been so many of them.

Because he was tall and exceedingly handsome the Marquis had been pursued by women ever since he had left school.

They found him irresistible.

Each one believed he would stay with her for ever, but unfortunately for them he soon became bored with each *affaire-de-coeur*.

Even he was sometimes shocked at how quickly it all came to an end.

When he met Lady Alsted, he had thought she was one of the most beautiful women he had ever come across and he naturally imagined that she would be different from all the others whose favours he had accepted.

However it was exactly the same scenario.

It had happened to him so often that he felt he knew the routine by heart.

There were the *rendezvous* they would arrange so that they would not be talked about.

If the husband was away or, as in the case of Lady Alsted, he was in the country having suffered a stroke, they had to be careful where they met.

He could only visit her when the entertainment for the evening was over and all the servants had gone to bed – half the gossip in Mayfair originated with the staff and they invariably knew what was happening in every house.

Even if they did not see who came in so late, they would have been told to leave the front door unbolted and this meant, of course, that the visitor had a key of his own.

The Marquis reached Park Lane, where his house was only a short distance away.

He had never expected that Silvia would want him to marry her.

He had grown so used to having love affairs with married women and their husbands were generally fishing, shooting or travelling abroad.

He had not, rather stupidly he now thought, taken into account that where Silvia was concerned her husband was seriously ill and likely to die.

Now, after all she had said to him this evening, he was aware that she was seeking marriage – which he had always shied away from.

He had witnessed very many of his contemporaries and friends married off to young girls, simply because their parents and hers had thought it a suitable match.

When he talked to them later, usually after only just a year or two of marriage, they had confided in him how incredibly bored they were.

Now the only possibility of having any amusement was to have a clandestine *affaire-de-coeur* with a married woman.

The great beauties of the *Beau Monde* were always available for the gentlemen of Society from the Prince of Wales downwards.

In fact, as the Marquis well knew, it was considered a privilege by most husbands for his wife to be pursued by His Royal Highness.

However, where the Marquis was concerned, it was the women who pursued him – not for his title, although it was an especially old one, but because he was undoubtedly the most handsome man in Mayfair – and the most cynical.

At twenty-eight he had been successful by sheer intuition and intelligence in avoiding the matrimonial traps that had been set for him – even by his elders who believed they were doing him a favour.

"I have found the right wife for you, Harlington," some distinguished older gentleman would say to him at a Reception or in White's Club.

They might even call at his own house and then the visitor would explain that his daughter, his niece or in the odd case his granddaughter was so incredibly beautiful and would be exactly the right chatelaine to sit at the end of the Marquis's table at Harlington Priory –

And in addition she would, of course, provide him with the necessary son to carry on his name.

He would realise why they had come almost before they began talking and when they received a rebuff, they would not only be upset but considered it an insult.

Yet on the whole he much preferred that approach to being embarrassed by endless ambitious mothers, who would try to pin him down and force him to listen to the amazing qualities of their daughters and how suitable they would be in providing him with an heir.

The Marquis was certainly wise enough never to be left alone with a young girl as he knew that he might easily be accused of ruining her reputation.

And he recognised only too well, he would then be obliged by the unwritten laws of English Society to make reparation and that meant asking for her hand in marriage.

So far he had managed by using his wits to remain a bachelor.

Only he knew how at times he had been in a tight corner and had only avoided a bride with what he called an 'inch to spare'.

Now as he reached his house in Park Lane, a night duty footman let him in.

He bowed respectfully, and the Marquis walked up the magnificent staircase towards the Master suite.

He never ordered his valet to wait up for him and as he undressed, he thought that to avoid a tearful scene with Silvia Alsted he must leave London.

And the quicker the better.

If there was one scene that really bored him, it was the tears and reproaches of those he had enjoyed himself with.

"What have I done?"

"Why do you no longer love me?"

"What has happened?"

"Who has caused mischief?"

He knew the questions only too well and made up his mind to avoid them at all costs.

This meant that he needed to go abroad or if it was the shooting season at least to Scotland.

Now at the end of May that exit was not available, so he wondered where he would particularly like to visit at this time of the year.

Paris was eternally enchanting and he had so often enjoyed himself there with its many irresistible *courtesans* and *cocottes*.

At the same time he resented having to leave his comfortable house in Park Lane and The Priory which was particularly lovely in the spring and summer.

Yet his major difficulty with the country was that, apart from riding there would be very little to do.

Later on in the autumn there was shooting and then hunting to fill up the days as well as house parties, which even without any hostess had been voted some of the most interesting and amusing at which the Prince of Wales had been a frequent guest.

But he had still not decided where he should go.

Because the Marquis was tired and his love-making with Silvia had been very fiery, he fell asleep quickly.

He was called at half-past eight as he had given no orders for it to be later.

The first letter he saw on the pile which had been put beside his place at the breakfast table was from No. 10 Downing Street.

He started to wonder why the Prime Minister, Mr. Benjamin Disraeli, was writing to him.

He had the uncomfortable feeling that he would be asking a favour of him.

'I am supplying no favours at the moment,' he told himself, 'and the sooner I leave London the better.'

By the time he had opened his other letters and read the newspapers it was nearly eleven o'clock.

He thought that as he had a luncheon engagement it would be best to see Mr. Disraeli first.

Forty minutes later the door of the Prime Minister's office opened and an official announced,

"The Marquis of Harlington has just arrived to see you, Prime Minister. Shall I ask his Lordship to step in?"

"Yes, of course."

Mr. Disraeli was sitting at his writing desk and rose when the Marquis entered, looking exceedingly smart.

It passed through the Prime Minister's mind that he looked as if there were no difficulties in his world.

"It is nice to see you again, Rex, and thank you for coming so quickly in answer to my letter."

"I imagine it must be urgent," replied the Marquis, "but if it means my journeying to some outlandish spot at a moment's notice, the answer is 'no'."

Mr. Disraeli laughed.

"It's not quite as bad as that!"

The Marquis sighed.

"I might have guessed that you did not want to see me without an ulterior motive behind the invitation!"

The Prime Minister did not answer, so he went on,

"As I have already intimated, I have no wish to visit some wild, obscure and uncivilised spot just because you are having a little difficulty with the natives."

The Prime Minister laughed again and then poured out a glass of champagne for him from a bottle in an ice-cooler in a corner of the room.

"It is really too early in the morning," the Marquis protested, "but I do see it is a particularly fine vintage, so it must not be wasted."

He sat down in a comfortable armchair opposite the fireplace and the Prime Minister sat down in another.

"What I am going to do now, Rex, is to ask you to help me in your usual brilliant way with a rather obtuse problem."

The Marquis groaned.

"I might have known it was what you had up your sleeve. But as I have already said, you know the answer."

"I think you might find this quite interesting, Rex. As far as I can remember, although I might be wrong, you have not been to Egypt for some time."

"*Egypt!*" exclaimed the Marquis.

"Yes, Egypt, I want you to find out for me what the current situation is concerning the Suez Canal that is now in the process of being built."

"I thought the English had decided a long time ago, Prime Minister, they would have nothing to do with it."

"Palmerston firmly opposed it from the beginning, saying that it would be to our commercial disadvantage, especially with regard to India."

"I remember that, but that fellow, de Lesseps, who organised the whole scheme, has persevered with it without our approval."

"He has indeed," Mr. Disraeli answered, "the Suez Canal is, in fact, nearly completed."

"Then we must at least commend him for sticking to his guns!"

The Marquis was well aware that although the idea of making a Canal through the Isthmus of Suez had often been proposed before, notably by Napoleon Bonaparte, it was only fourteen years ago that Mr. Ferdinand de Lesseps produced a practical scheme for constructing such a Canal.

He was a French Diplomat who was in retirement,

but he had been brought up in Egypt where his father was the French Consul.

Apparently since boyhood he had been fired with enthusiasm for a French project of carving a Canal through the Suez Isthmus, but the Sultan's Viceroy at the time had refused to countenance such an idea.

When the Sultan was murdered after only six years rule, his place had been taken by his young son Saïd, who was incompetent and clownish.

He had been educated in Paris where de Lesseps had helped to tutor him and as soon as he heard that Saïd was now in power, de Lesseps had caught the first ship for Egypt.

And he received a warm welcome from his former pupil.

The Marquis was recalling all this without speaking as Mr. Disraeli, with his amazing Jewish perception, which was to help him all through his life, remarked,

"I thought perhaps you would remember that Saïd was supposed to have signed de Lesseps' draft concession for the construction of the Canal without even reading it."

The Marquis laughed.

"Yes, I had heard that story and I was also told that he had made a bad deal for Egypt."

"We were told so at the time," the Prime Minister agreed, "as Saïd had disposed of two strips of land for the Canal, only one side being rich, because it received fresh water from the Nile."

The Marquis was listening intently, but there was a look on his face that told the Prime Minister he was still going to refuse to do whatever he was asked.

"You must indeed remember, Rex, how everyone was horrified when works began in 1855 with de Lesseps himself wielding the first pickaxe on the sand dunes."

"And the labourers who followed were slaves – "

"Exactly," the Prime Minister concurred. "And all twenty thousand of them were driven by the courbash."

The Marquis knew that the courbash was a whip of hippopotamus-hide which, when used on the backs of men, caused the most dreadful agony.

"It was not surprising we protested, Prime Minister, but if I remember rightly Saïd refused to listen."

"That is correct, Rex, and when in 1862 the Canal reached as far as Lake Timsah, de Lesseps invited a large gathering of the Moslem and Catholic faiths – "

He paused for a moment as if he was looking back into the past and then he continued,

"De Lesseps then actually said, '*in the name of His Highness Mohammed Saïd, I command that the waters of the Mediterranean now enter Lake Timsah by the Grace of God*'."

"I would have thought that he might have included the wretched slaves who had suffered so acutely in making it possible."

"I agree with you, Rex, but perhaps it was an act of Divine justice that Saïd died a year later of an incurable disease!"

"Yes, I recall that now, Prime Minister, and he was succeeded by his nephew Ismail, who is now the Khedive."

"That is right. He is ugly, short and ungainly, but I have met him and he has an extraordinary charm which, combined with the inherited shrewdness of his ancestors, has served him well up to now."

"What is the problem?" the Marquis asked. "The Canal is nearly finished and there is no point in the English going on being disagreeable about it."

"The problem really is that de Lesseps has now run out of money. The British Government under Russell after Palmerston's death was more amenable to the project."

The Marquis nodded to show he remembered as the Prime Minister continued,

"Ismail is presently touring Europe reporting news of the Canal's progress to Heads of State, pressing them to attend the Opening Ceremony next year."

The Marquis laughed.

"Well, he has succeeded, or rather de Lesseps has, and we can be pleased that it has not cost us anything."

"That is where you are wrong, Rex. I agree that I was against the idea in the beginning, but now I think that the Canal could be an advantage rather than a disadvantage to England."

The Marquis stared at him.

"You are doing a complete about-turn – "

The Prime Minister sighed.

"I opposed the building of the Suez Canal almost as strongly as Palmerston, but I must be honest and recognise now that it could be of great use as the gateway to India."

"You astound me, Prime Minister."

"Sometimes I rather astound myself, Rex, but I am worried and depressed that I was not wise enough to realise the possibility at the very beginning. In fact, what I want now is shares in the Suez Canal for Great Britain!"

The Marquis stared at him in further astonishment.

"I never thought I would hear you say that – "

"I am being honest as I have always been. I made a mistake and I now admit that the Canal is essential for us and India. If we cannot obtain complete control of it, we might at least prevent it going wholly to the French.

"I now understand that new shares will be offered and what I want you to find out is what will be their price and if it is possible for us to purchase them."

"I will do my best," the Marquis responded. "But as usual you have given me an extremely difficult task. I suppose we can only hope that we can find a way to make amends for the past British opposition to the Canal."

The Prime Minister nodded as if it was impossible to put what he felt into words.

"Very well, Prime Minister, I will go to Egypt and see what I can find out. But, as you know, the French are extremely greedy and, if they have a hold on the Canal at this moment, they will not give it up to us of all people."

"You are surely right, Rex, but I have a feeling in my bones that sooner or later the French will find it too costly a project and that is where we could come in."

"What I will need," added the Marquis, "more than anything else is to take a good interpreter with me. I don't speak any Arabic and I imagine if they are really having difficulties they will not shout it from the rooftops."

"You are quite right, at the same time interpreters in Arabic are difficult to find. And if he travels with you, he must be so careful what he says in front of others."

The Marquis laughed.

"That is only too true. But do your best to find one for me as I would intend to leave in three days time."

The Prime Minister was obviously delighted as he had expected that the Marquis would refuse to go until the Season had come to an end.

He imagined the reason was a feminine one, but he was too polite to ask questions, so he merely remarked,

"I am deeply grateful to you, Rex. You have never failed your country in the past and I just cannot believe you will fail me now."

"Do not be too optimistic, Prime Minister."

"I am sure that there will be many difficulties. The worst of them, of course, being those who live just across the Channel."

"So true, Prime Minister, and naturally de Lesseps, being a Frenchman, will always give preference to his own countrymen over ours."

When the Marquis left No. 10 Downing Street, he felt that he had committed himself.

Equally he would undoubtedly find his mission so much more interesting than just wandering around Europe seeking another beauty to take Silvia Alsted's place.

This was what he had done in similar circumstances in the past.

*

When he arrived back at his house in Park Lane, he instructed his butler that he would be leaving immediately for Harlington Priory.

And he was also to inform the Captain of his yacht that he was to be ready to put to sea on Saturday.

"You're leaving us, my Lord!" the butler exclaimed in surprise.

"I have an important engagement abroad, Cheshunt, which I have to keep, but I will not be away for too long."

"I do hope not, my Lord, as your Lordship has two horses running at Royal Ascot and everyone in the house is backing them."

"Then I would hope they will not be disappointed, Cheshunt, and if I am not back in time to see them run, you must cheer them on my behalf."

He walked upstairs and Cheshunt stared after him with a concerned look in his eyes.

He had known the Marquis since he was a small boy and was very fond of him, as were all the household.

He only hoped that his Lordship was not in trouble, yet he rather suspected he might be and that actually would not be a surprise.

The Marquis drove down to the country with a team of his fastest horses.

They were all perfectly matched stallions and were obviously delighted to leave London.

The Marquis was not as enthusiastic as they were, but at the same time he knew that he had to leave because of Silvia Alsted.

It was easier to have a valid excuse rather than to invent one.

He also had no wish to see Silvia again and he was certain it would all result in another tearful scene.

He had thus written her a most affectionate note, thanking her for the happiness she had given him and how sorry he was to be going abroad for a vital engagement that could not be postponed.

He did not explain what it was about or where he was going and he reckoned that if she did write to him, as women always did, his secretary would keep any letters for his return.

By then, with any luck, she would have discovered some other gentleman to amuse her and in time he would be forgotten.

Fortunately Harlington Priory was only about two and a half hours drive from London.

On the way he remembered that he would have to communicate with one of his neighbours, as he would be unable to attend the dinner party Lord Durham was giving when he had promised to make a speech.

The occasion had been planned for some time and concerned the complete repair and enlargement of the local Racecourse – for generations the people of Hertfordshire had raced their horses on it.

It was the Marquis supported by Lord Durham, who had taken up the idea and promised to raise the necessary funds.

As the Marquis was enjoying himself in London, Lord Durham, who preferred the country, had in the past few months done all the necessary work.

Lord Durham had arranged for the dinner party at his house to inform his neighbours about developments and these included new stables for the horses and a new stand.

'Durham will be so annoyed with me,' the Marquis thought, 'but if I give him a larger cheque than I originally intended, he will be happy to take my place.'

Actually he disliked Lord Durham and would have much preferred to work with someone else in the County, but Lord Durham's estate bordered his and he was the Lord Lieutenant.

Thus Lord Durham was more important officially than anyone else in the County.

The Marquis's father had been Lord Lieutenant for the last twenty years of his life and when he died his son was thought too young, in the Queen's opinion, to follow immediately in his father's footsteps.

Then Lord Durham, to his utmost satisfaction, had been appointed and the Marquis was certain that he would continue in office until he was carried to his grave.

When the Marquis arrived at The Priory, he thought it was looking even more beautiful than it usually did.

It had been built in the reign of Henry VII and with the Dissolution of the Monasteries it had then fallen into the hands of the Earls of Harlington.

It was as the ninth Earl that the Marquis had been rewarded by Queen Victoria the previous year and created the first Marquis.

He was being thanked for what he had done for Her Majesty in India, where he had not only saved the lives of many soldiers, but prevented an uprising when it had been least expected.

It had been fomented by Russian interference and it was more by good luck than anything else that the Marquis had been in that part of India when the incident occurred.

It was only by his quickness of thought that it had been possible to forestall a damaging revolution that would have wiped out the small British contingent stationed there.

It was entirely thanks to his initiative and his innate bravery that disaster had been avoided.

Because it was considered a mistake for people to talk too much about the incident, the Viceroy had thought that the best way to reward the Marquis was to appeal to Queen Victoria.

She had appreciated clearly what was expected of her and she made him the first Marquis of Harlington when he had not yet reached his twenty-seventh birthday.

Naturally he was delighted and honoured, but found that his new title carried a great deal more responsibility.

Now he was only concerned with tidying up ends at home whilst he was away for what he hoped would only be a short period of time.

He told his secretary to keep an eye on everything on the estate and he knew that the old servants would keep the house as perfect and safe during his absence as they did when they expected him to drop in at any time.

He went to bed quite late, having found that there were a number of decisions to be made about the estate.

The Marquis woke early and rode before breakfast.

He enjoyed galloping over his own land and taking the jumps that were familiar to him ever since he had first rode a spirited horse of his own.

After breakfast he ordered the special team which drew his up-to-date chaise to be waiting for him at twelve o'clock.

"I am going to call on Lord Durham and I will not return when I leave him, but will drive straight to London," he told the butler.

"Take good care of yourself, my Lord, and we'll all be waiting anxiously till you gets back."

"I know, Dawkins, that all will look as it does now. And do tell your wife that dinner last night was delicious. I don't suppose I will eat a better one until I return."

Dawkins, who was over sixty, smiled.

"That's what we want to hear, Master Rex – I mean my Lord, and I promise nothing'll go wrong while you are away."

"I know I can depend on you, Dawkins."

He climbed into his chaise and drove towards Lord Durham's house – which he thought inferior to his own – it had been built at the start of the century and at the time was hailed as modern and up-to-date.

Lord Durham had spent a great deal of money on it and on the vast garden that surrounded it, but the Marquis had often thought he was jealous of The Priory.

Simply because it was unique and very much older than any other house in the County and the family tree of the Harlingtons was unquestionably respected by everyone.

The Marquis drove along the country lanes thinking as he did so that he was quite content when he was at The Priory to be on his own.

Whatever his relations might say to him, he had no intention of marrying anyone.

'Perhaps when I am forty, I will think differently,' he reflected, 'but for the moment at least it is a question of 'he who travels fastest, travels alone'.'

He then turned in at Lord Durham's rather ugly and over-decorated gates and drove up the long drive towards Durham House.

Every time he visited it, he thought how incredibly unattractive it was compared to The Priory.

If he had been asked to design a house for the Lord Lieutenant of Hertfordshire, he could most certainly have provided a more handsome and attractive one.

The Marquis was not expected but the butler bowed him respectfully into a sitting room.

He said he would find his Lordship who he thought was in the garden.

When the Marquis was left alone he considered that the room was rather gloomy and everything about it was too new to be of any particular interest.

Because it was hot and rather stuffy in the room, he opened one of the French windows to let in some air – the garden at least, he had to admit, was well laid out and the flowers themselves were most colourful.

As he took a step further forward to go outside, he was aware of voices emanating from a window to his left.

To his astonishment he heard Lord Durham's voice shouting,

"If I have to beat you till you are unconscious, you *will* marry the Comte."

"I am too old to be beaten now, Papa, as you beat me when I was a child," a soft little voice responded.

"*I am not joking*," Lord Durham screamed. "It is a

great honour that the Comte should ask for your hand in marriage and I have given him my *full* approval. And now I will have no arguments about it!"

"But I am the one who has to marry him, Papa," the girl protested. "As you well know, he is not French but Egyptian and there is something horrid and beastly about him."

"You are talking complete and utter nonsense," said Lord Durham furiously. "I do believe the Comte's mother was an Egyptian, but he has large properties in France, and you should be pleased, in fact delighted, that any man of his importance and his wealth should wish to marry *you*."

"He is old, ugly and unpleasant and why should I want his money?" the girl riposted with spirit.

"If you don't want it, I do!" Lord Durham answered coldly. "He is most generous and exactly the sort of son-in-law I require. He is coming here this very evening and you will accept him and be married as soon as it is possible for the nuptials to be arranged."

"*I refuse*! I utterly refuse, Papa! I hate him and it makes me creep even to see him. I would rather die than let him touch me."

There was a sincerity in the girl's voice the Marquis found very touching.

Then there was a hard sound and a scream and he reckoned that Lord Durham had struck his daughter.

If there was one thing the Marquis disliked, it was cruelty of any sort.

For a moment he contemplated hammering on the window to tell Lord Durham to stop bullying the poor girl for standing up to him.

Then as he struck her again there was yet another scream.

The door into the room must then have opened, for he heard the butler intoning,

"The Marquis of Harlington's waiting to see you, my Lord."

"Harlington! I wonder what he wants?"

Then Lord Durham shouted at his daughter,

"If I have hurt you, it is what you deserve. Tonight you will meet the Comte and accept his offer of marriage."

There was no answer but a sob from the girl.

The Marquis then moved quickly back through the French window and into the room he had just left.

He felt desperately sorry for the girl who was being treated in such a horrible way by her odious father.

But it was none of his business and he recognised that he had no right to interfere.

At the same time it made him dislike Lord Durham even more than he did already.

A moment later the door opened and Lord Durham walked in smiling and holding out his hand.

"How delightful it is to see you, Harlington. I was wondering when you would be home and when we would have a chance of talking again about the Racecourse."

"I have just come here to see you to tell you that unfortunately I have to go abroad for a short time and I will therefore have to miss the dinner party you have arranged."

"Miss it?" Lord Durham queried. "I cannot believe it! You know I have been planning it for months and it is most important that you should be present."

"I know, and I can only say how terribly sorry I am to behave so badly, but you will understand that it is not a journey of pleasure, but one of *duty*."

He spoke in the sort of knowing voice which made

Lord Durham nod his head in agreement as if he was used to such situations.

"Naturally I do understand, my dear boy, but at the same time we will miss you."

"I feel sure that you will say how sorry I am not to be present," added the Marquis, "and I am quite prepared to start the fund with a cheque for two thousand pounds."

Because he was not expecting it Lord Durham gave a little gasp.

"That is indeed generous of you, Harlington, very generous, and I am sure everyone will be most impressed. Obviously I hope that they too will open their purses."

"I hope so too and I have brought some papers with me that will tell you what my people have estimated all the construction work will cost."

"Thank you, thank you," said Lord Durham. "I will read them very carefully and discuss them with you when you return. Will you be away for long?"

"No, only a short time, Durham, I cannot give you an exact date, but I will want to see my horses running at Royal Ascot."

Lord Durham chortled.

"Yes, of course, you must not miss Ascot."

"I am sorry to have to be so tiresome and if there is anything you need from The Priory, my secretary will be only too willing to supply it for you."

"That will be most useful. Now let me offer you a drink."

The Marquis shook his head.

"No, it is too early in the morning and I am actually on my way to London."

"I had no idea you were at The Priory."

"I only arrived last night to make sure everything was in order and to tell the servants that I will be away, but my old staff, who were all with my father, keep things fully shipshape whether I am here or not."

"Certainly, Harlington, and let me thank you again for your most generous cheque. I will, I promise, make it clear to all those present how sorry you are not to be with us in person."

"Thank you very much."

He walked to the door and Lord Durham opened it for him.

As they walked into the hall, the Marquis saw that his horses were waiting outside and the groom who had run from the stables when he had arrived was still standing at their heads.

He shook hands with Lord Durham and walked to the back of his carriage.

As he did so he hesitated for a moment.

Then jumping into the driving seat he picked up the reins and as Lord Durham waved he set off down the drive.

He was thinking as he drove away of the pathetic girl he had overheard crying out in her childlike voice as her vicious father tried to beat her into submission.

# CHAPTER TWO

The Marquis drove for about three miles away from Lord Durham's house.

Then he turned off the road into a small wood and up a rough track running between the trees.

He pulled the horses to a standstill as they could go no further.

He fixed his reins, climbed out and walked round to the back of his chaise.

The fragment of blue ribbon he had noticed on his departure was still hanging out of the box that was there to hold luggage or extra rugs for cold weather.

He pulled open the door and said quietly,

"You can come out now."

A small frightened face looked up at him.

He recognised that it was the face of someone very young yet exceedingly beautiful.

She stared at him.

Then she asked in a soft childlike voice,

"How – did you know – I was here?"

"Before I got into the driving seat, I saw a piece of your sash sticking out."

There was no reply.

"It must be extremely uncomfortable in that box, I suggest you come and sit in the front of the chaise with me and tell me where you want to go."

She looked at him and her eyes searched his face as if to ask if she could trust him.

Then she stammered,

"You are not – taking me – back?"

"Not unless you want to – "

She crawled forward and the Marquis then helped her onto the ground.

"I suggest we sit more comfortably in the chaise."

She did not answer but climbed onto the seat beside him.

"Now tell me where do you think you are going?"

"I have run away from Papa," the girl murmured.

"I do realise that. In fact I heard you crying when I was waiting to see him."

"Did you hear – why I was crying?"

"I understood that your father wants you to marry someone you have no intention of marrying. But I do not think running away will really solve your problem."

"It will – if you will take me to London – "

He had noticed as he was talking to her that there was a red bruise on her cheek where her father had hit her.

"I will take you to London, if you have any friends there you can stay with."

"What I really want," the girl said hesitatingly, "is a – Convent."

"A Convent!" ejaculated the Marquis.

"Yes, because if I become a nun – Papa will not be able to marry me off to some terrible man like – the one he has chosen for me."

The Marquis, who was sitting sideways so that he could look at her, stared at her in disbelief.

It seemed incredible that this young and very lovely girl would prefer to become a nun in a Convent rather than marry anyone however unpleasant.

She looked at him beseechingly as her eyes filled with tears until finally he suggested,

"Let's start at the beginning. You very likely know that I am the Marquis of Harlington and that I live nearby at The Priory, but I do not know your name."

"It is – Delisia."

The Marquis smiled.

"A very appropriate name, but certainly not suitable for a Convent!"

"What else can I do?" Delisia asked spreading out her hands.

"You must have some relatives. Surely they will be pleased to see you."

"The only relatives I have are scared of Papa and he gives them allowances so they certainly would not quarrel with him."

The Marquis found it difficult to know what to say next and finally he enquired,

"How old are you?"

"I am eighteen."

"Well, you look much younger."

She did not answer immediately, but then she said,

"*Please* find me a Convent – or somewhere where I can hide. But, as you will understand, I came away just as I was when I saw your chaise – and I have no other clothes or money with me."

"I can easily provide that, Delisia, but I want to be quite certain you are doing the right thing in defying your father."

He glanced again at the mark on her cheek while he remembered the loud scream she had given when her father struck her.

"What I wish to find out is if there is anyone who could talk to your father and make him understand that you cannot marry this man you have taken such a dislike to."

"He is horrible! Horrible!" Delisia cried. "He is a Comte with a large château in France which has impressed Papa, but he is also half Egyptian and I am sure – he has a harem somewhere in the East!"

"What on earth makes you think that?"

Delisia looked away from him, before answering,

"I was reading about Sultans in the East – and I am quite certain, although Papa will not listen to me – that the Comte is more Eastern in his ways – than any Frenchman."

The words came hesitatingly from her as if she felt embarrassed at having to say them.

The Marquis was wondering what on earth he could possibly do.

After all, this child – she was nothing more – was exquisitively beautiful.

But he had heard her father threatening to beat her.

How could he take her back to him to suffer as she had suffered already from the merciless blow to her cheek.

Then he picked up the reins and started to back his horses out of the wood.

"*Please*, please – you are not going to take me back to – Papa?" Delisia pleaded in a terrified voice.

"Of course I wouldn't without your agreement," the Marquis assured her. "But I am wondering what I will do with you and which of my many relatives could possibly take care of you."

She did not answer and he continued,

"When your father finds out that you are missing, he will undoubtedly then suspect me of spiriting you away. There was no other carriage at the house and you obviously came away with just the clothes you stand up in."

"It was my only chance, my Lord, as the Comte is coming this evening – to stay for a night or two with Papa – and arrange the marriage."

"Tell me, why do you dislike this Comte so much?"

By now they were on a straight piece of road and the horses had increased their pace.

"As I have said, he is not really French at all and although Papa thinks he is a friend, I heard him say to his valet, 'that old man is a stupid fool'."

"You heard him say that!" the Marquis exclaimed. "Was he speaking in French?"

"No he was speaking in Arabic and the valet replied in the same language, 'I agree with Your Highness, but all Englishmen are exactly like that, stupid and puffed up with their own self-importance'."

"You heard the valet speak in Arabic as well?" the Marquis asked her in a surprised voice.

"He went on saying a lot more, but I crept away in case they should realise that I had overheard them, not that they would think for a moment that I understood them."

"Are you really telling me," the Marquis enquired, "that you speak Arabic?"

For the first time Delisia smiled.

"Does it seem so very strange to you? As it happens I just love learning languages and I speak French, German, Italian and Greek. Then, when I was at school in Paris last year, a girl came from Egypt and she was the daughter of a businessman in Luxor and spoke very little English."

"So you learnt Arabic from her?"

Delisia nodded.

"We shared a room and so I taught her English and she taught me Arabic. It was a fair exchange."

"And you are really fluent in the Arabic language?" the Marquis asked her keenly.

"I found that it was easy to learn and I could soon understand everything Emili said to me. Actually she was very slow in learning English."

It struck the Marquis that this was an extraordinary coincidence – one which perhaps had been sent to him as a gift from Heaven.

At the same time and for his own sake, he had to be cautious.

"Are you absolutely certain, Delisia, that you have nowhere to go to in London and that I cannot take you to a friend or a relative who could hide you from your father?"

"If there was one – I promise you I would tell you. But my relatives, who live mostly in the country, are, as I have already said, terrified of Papa and under an obligation to him. If I went to them tonight, Papa would undoubtedly arrive to fetch me away tomorrow morning and the Comte – would be waiting for me."

There was terror in her voice that the Marquis could not misunderstand.

Yet he had to be certain.

"So your only possible plan is to become a nun?"

"I do not really want to be shut up in a Convent," Delisia admitted, "but anything would be better than to be married to that horrible beastly man. I would much rather – die than let him – touch me."

The Marquis was silent.

They drove for quite a long way before he spoke,

"I have been thinking over your predicament and I have a proposition to put to you. But it involves taking a risk not only by you, but by me."

He was aware as he spoke that Delisia had turned towards him eagerly.

She looked at him almost as if he was coming down from Heaven in a chariot of fire to rescue her.

'She is incredibly lovely,' he thought warily, 'and lovely women *always* cause trouble.'

At the same time she was not really a woman – it was not only her voice that was childlike, but she did not look at all grown-up.

Her hands were very small and he needed to use the word again – *childlike*.

He realised Delisia was waiting for him to speak, so he carried on,

"By some strange coincidence I am leaving tonight in my yacht and I am sailing to see the new Canal which is being built in the Suez Isthmus. What I have asked for, but have not been able to find, is an interpreter."

He glanced at Delisia.

Her eyes had now opened so wide that they seemed to fill her whole face.

They were not the same shade of blue as Silvia's, which were the darkest of blue that could only light up in passion.

Instead Delisia's eyes were the very pale blue of the early forget-me-not or the sky in the early morning when the sun was just breaking through.

"Are you saying, my Lord," she asked in a voice he could hardly decipher, "that you would take me with you to Egypt?"

"I certainly would find you useful, but equally we would both be taking great risks."

He knew that Delisia was listening and he went on,

"I am running away for almost the same reason as you are!"

He could appreciate that she did not understand him and so he explained,

"There is a woman in my life who wants to marry me and I have no wish to be married."

"Then you understand what I am feeling, my Lord."

"Of course I do. No one who has any intelligence wants to be pressured into marrying someone they do not love – when they know instinctively, as you and I do, that the marriage would be an utter disaster."

"Naturally – it would," she agreed. "To be married one must really love someone – otherwise it would all be a complete misery."

She spoke with pain in her voice.

"That is just why we must both now escape!" the Marquis exclaimed.

"Then you will really take me with you, my Lord?"

"I am just thinking how it could be possible. You do realise, because you are intelligent, that if it is known that I have a beautiful young woman with me on my yacht, many will assume that we have a certain relationship with each other and, when we finally return back home, to save your reputation, I will surely be forced to marry you."

There was silence and then Delisia murmured in a very different voice,

"Are you saying – you cannot take me?"

"No, what I am saying, Delisia, is that we have to be very clever about it all. To begin with it would be most reprehensible of me, if I am on a special mission, to arrive with a beautiful woman who is not chaperoned."

"Perhaps when we actually arrive in Egypt, I could – hide myself, my Lord?"

"A better idea has come into my mind, but you may not like it."

"I would like any plan that will take me away from Papa at this moment – and the dreadful man he has chosen for my husband."

"You told me just now you are eighteen, but you certainly look much younger. What I am going to suggest, although you may not like it, is that you travel with me as my niece and you will behave and dress just as if you were a girl of fifteen. It should not be too difficult."

Delisia clasped her hands together.

"That is wonderful, wonderful of you! If you take me with you, I swear I will help you and do everything you ask of me, my Lord, however difficult."

"The problem is that no one must find out you are *not* my niece."

"Then you – will take me with you, my Lord? Oh, thank you! Thank you! How could you be so marvellous? How could God have sent you to me when I was feeling so desperate and – thinking I must die?"

"You must never think of anything like that again," scolded the Marquis. "You are young, beautiful and have your whole life in front of you."

"I know that," Delisia replied, "but I ran away from Papa, because he threatened to beat me and I am sure he would have hit me again if the butler had not come to say you had arrived. I felt I would much rather jump into the lake – than have to marry that Comte."

"Life is very precious," the Marquis counselled her,

"and however bad it becomes, you must never again think of taking your own life."

"I know it was wrong of me, my Lord, then I saw your chaise outside the front door, and I remembered there was a hiding-place in the back of chaises which I had once used when I was playing hide-and-seek."

"So you climbed in, Delisia, and I am only hoping that the groom who was holding my horses' heads was not aware of it."

"Ben is a stupid boy. He loves horses and is always talking to them instead of getting on with his work. He was talking to your two leading horses and I don't think he would have noticed if a firework had gone off in the garden or in front of the house!"

The Marquis laughed.

"Are you quite certain no one else saw you?"

"Just in case they did, my Lord, please drive a little faster, so that if Papa is coming behind us, he will not be able to catch us up."

This, the Marquis thought, was sensible.

His team was a splendidly fast one and as far as he could recall, Lord Durham's horses were usually rather fat and slow.

They drove much faster for a little while before the Marquis commented drily,

"I suppose you realise, Delisia, you have no clothes to wear."

"I was just thinking of that myself, but I thought it would annoy you if I reminded you of the problem."

"Well, you can scarcely travel with me to Egypt in what you are wearing, and as I am determined to leave this evening, you will have to find a shop very rapidly."

"I will be as quick as I can, but have you any idea where there is a shop where we can buy clothes suitable for a girl of fifteen?"

The Marquis thought.

"What we really need is a shop where you can buy everything."

"You do realise," Delisia added a little hesitantly, "that I have no money?"

"You need not worry about money. I will be quite prepared to dress my interpreter, whether it is a man or a woman!"

"If I was really your niece aged fifteen, my Lord, I would be neatly and quietly dressed."

"Quite right. You must not be at all eye-catching or even smart. In fact the less people notice you, the better."

As he spoke he realised how lovely she was and he knew that it was no use pretending that she would not be noticed and admired wherever she went.

It was then that the Marquis noticed that her hair was drawn back into a bun at the back of her head.

"When you were fifteen," he enquired, "you did not wear your hair pinned back as it is now."

Delisia gave a little cry.

"How very clever of you, my Lord, and how stupid of me not to think of it. Of course my hair was long and I did not tie it back until I was a year older."

She pulled at her hair and then took out a number of hairpins.

Then he could see that her golden hair was indeed long and fell down in cascades over her shoulders as far as her breasts.

It waved naturally and as it caught the sunlight, he

thought that nothing could look quite so innocent and yet alluring.

At the same time it made her seem much younger.

He was astute enough to know that no one glancing at her would think she was a day over fifteen years of age.

As they drove on he thought of his past adventures – there had been a great number of them – but this was one of the most extraordinary and perhaps the most foolish.

But equally it went against every grain in his body to abandon this young child to a horrible fate.

She would be beaten by her father and forced into marriage with a man much older than herself who was not even of the same nationality.

If she really could speak fluent Arabic, she would be exceedingly useful to him.

Who would ever suspect for a moment that a child would be his interpreter?

They drove on for a little while as the Marquis was thinking out his plan of campaign.

Only when they had not spoken for nearly twenty minutes did Delisia pipe up,

"You are not changing your mind, my Lord?"

"No, of course not. I was just thinking things out. We must make it clear to everyone including the crew and the Stewards on-board that you really are my niece. There is just one exception as there is only one person who will do everything I want and who I would trust with my life."

"Who is that?" Delisia asked apprehensively.

It flashed through her mind that perhaps, after what he had said, there would be a lady aboard his yacht.

If he was taken with her, she might well be irritated at his bringing another woman aboard – she might be only a child, but the lady concerned would want him to herself.

Then to her relief the Marquis explained,

"I am actually speaking about my valet. Hutton has been with me since I was a young boy, and he and I have been in some very strange places and tough situations. He will be the only person aboard *The Scimitar* who I would trust to know who you really are."

He smiled before he added,

"Having been with me so long, he knows I have no niece because, as it happens, I was an only child."

"Just like me, my Lord, I have often thought what fun it would be to have a brother. I always envied the girls at school when they talked about their large families."

"Well, if you have not had a brother, you will have to put up with an uncle!"

"And a very kind and wonderful uncle, who came to my rescue when I was really desperate. When I say my prayers tonight, I will thank God over and over again that I found you and that you have been so kind to me."

"Don't thank me just yet, Delisia, we have a lot of jumps ahead of us before we finally leave England. Only when we are a long way out to sea in *The Scimitar* will we be certain that you have escaped what would undoubtedly be a disastrous marriage."

He thought as he spoke that the very same applied to himself.

He could think of nothing worse than being married to Silvia and as he knew only too well he would soon find her a bore and would start to look for new adventures.

He was fully aware of the feeling of boredom that already crept over him when he arranged to see her.

If she was his wife, it would be quite impossible to escape as he was doing now.

In fact luck was treating him almost too generously.

The Prime Minister's request that he should go to Egypt had come at exactly the right moment.

And now the answer to his need for an interpreter had dropped down like Manna from Heaven.

He realised that he would be heavily handicapped if he was unable to understand the language of Egypt.

*

They drove on for over an hour and when they were passing through a small town, the Marquis noticed a square where there were a number of expensive-looking shops.

Almost instinctively he slowed his horses down and then he came to a standstill outside a shop that displayed a collection of ladies' clothes in the window.

"Shall we try in here for your clothes, Delisia?"

To his surprise she shook her head.

"No?" he questioned.

"This is only a small town, my Lord, and you have caused much attention already with your outstanding team of horses – you also look very smart and rich!"

The Marquis had to admit that she was right.

"If we do shop here," Delisia continued, "you will undoubtedly be remembered and if Papa makes enquiries and your description is given to him, he will know at once it was *you*."

"That is true and very bright of you, Delisia."

The Marquis then drove his team rapidly out of the town and once again they were on their way to London.

He thought as he left the houses behind that Delisia certainly had brains – and that was more than he expected from most girls of her age or any age for that matter.

He had always taken a dislike to the endless stream of *debutantes* giggling with each other around the ballroom or being paraded in front of him by their ambitious mothers in the forlorn hope that he would find them attractive.

He had even on some occasions been asked outright if he would care to dance with a *debutante* and had always managed to make some excuse, as he knew he would have nothing in common with her, however pretty she might be.

Yet here was a young girl who really did look only fifteen years old and was almost teaching him his job.

In fact he prided himself on being extremely clever at disguises, especially at appearing to be just an ordinary man of no standing rather than himself.

"Yes," he repeated, "very bright of you. For I am afraid that when your father cannot find you, he is bound to suspect that I have taken you away."

"There was no one else calling at home today but the Comte," Delisia answered, "and he is not expected until nearly dinner-time."

"Do you really think your father will follow us to London?"

"I am hoping that he will realise too late, in fact just before the Comte arrives, that I am not in the house. He is used to my running away to hide after he has beaten me or screaming at me about something I have done."

"When did your mother die, Delisia?"

"It seems a long time ago now, but actually it was only three years ago. I miss her terribly. She was the only person who could make Papa kinder and less cruel to me. But even she could not stop him beating me when I would not do something he wanted me to do."

She spoke quite naturally and yet there was a little sob in her voice and the Marquis knew it was because her mother was no longer with her.

As if she realised he was interested, she went on,

"It was Mama who persuaded Papa to send me to the Finishing School in Paris. She knew I was interested in other countries and languages and I was very happy there."

"You did not think of returning to your school and asking them to hide you from your father?"

"I did not consider it. I know that they could not by law keep me against my father's wish, and it would be very embarrassing for them if I begged them to hide me, which they would feel they ought not to do."

"So, if I had not turned up – ?" he began to ask and then he stopped, remembering what the alternative might have been.

"I am not afraid of dying," Delisia asserted. "But I feel it would be rather a waste and I have always believed that God would send me off on an adventure like this one, although I could not think how it could possibly happen."

"This will certainly be an adventure as soon as we can sail away," the Marquis promised.

*

Later when they were on the outskirts of London he said,

"Now do keep your eyes open for a large outfitting shop to provide you with everything you need. Although, of course, we could stop when we reach France or Italy."

"I still think I had better have at least a nightgown to wear, my Lord, and you will become extremely tired of this dress if you see it every day at breakfast, luncheon, tea and dinner!"

The Marquis laughed as she meant him to do.

"Actually it is most attractive, Delisia, but I would suppose it might be a little monotonous. In any case you must be dressed in such a manner that the Captain and the crew accept that you are only fifteen."

They were now driving in the Northern suburbs of the City and they came to a street lined with shops, among them a large establishment with bow windows displaying a variety of women's clothes.

"I think that will be a safe shop to visit, my Lord, as there is a place for the horses outside and they will not be too surprised at your smart appearance."

The Marquis drew his horses to an abrupt standstill and then he noticed a young lad who was obviously hoping to be given a chance to look after them.

He touched his forelock and looked at the Marquis pleadingly.

"As I have some shopping to do," the Marquis said, "I will leave my horses in your charge, but be very careful to hold them steadily and not let them move about."

"I'm used to 'orses, sir."

The boy patted the first of the team as he spoke and the Marquis knew it to be a good sign.

"We will not be very long, boy, but if you find you are in any trouble, send someone in to ask for me."

"Yessir."

They walked into the shop that had quite a number of expensive items on show.

A woman came forward.

"Is there anything I can do for you, sir."

"I want to speak to the Manager or Manageress, my name is the Marquis of Harlington and I am in a hurry."

"I will fetch the Manager immediately, my Lord."

The woman scurried into the back of the shop.

An elderly man, well-dressed and with an educated voice, came towards them.

"I am the Marquis of Harlington," the Marquis said again, "and my niece, whom I have just collected from her school, has unfortunately been robbed of all her luggage. As we are leaving tonight for the Continent, I want you to fit her out at once with everything she will need."

"What you ask, my Lord, is not difficult, and I can promise we'll be as quick as we possibly can."

He called four women who were serving behind the counters and told them what was required.

Then he asked the Marquis and Delisia to come into the back of the shop where there was a changing room.

The Marquis kept glancing at his watch and they were obviously impressed by him.

In what seemed a short time Delisia was provided with a number of pretty girl's dresses, most of which were in white with a coloured sash.

There were two coats to wear in case she was cold, besides several nightgowns and a dressing gown.

Other more intimate garments Delisia chose herself without the Marquis's involvement. However, he approved of some pairs of shoes and several pretty straw hats.

Watching her choose what she wanted, the Marquis recognised that she had very good taste and was extremely intelligent.

He had told her she would be travelling in a yacht and she therefore insisted on two dresses that were warmer than the one she was wearing as well as suitable shoes for a heaving deck.

He was aware that she had very determined ideas of her own as to what she should and should not wear – and anything that was obviously too fussy or unsuitable for a girl of fifteen she waved away.

Less than an hour later they went outside with the clothes packed in two suitcases which they had been able to buy at the shop as well.

The Marquis had written out a large cheque for all the clothes they had bought.

Delisia was already wearing one of the new young girl's dresses as the Marquis had suggested so that he could introduce her convincingly as his niece when they boarded the yacht.

The Manager bowed them off the premises with all expressions of gratitude.

To the Marquis's relief his team was still waiting, apparently quite unperturbed, and the boy who had looked after them was so heavily tipped he was almost speechless with surprise and pleasure.

"It was perhaps rather dangerous," he admitted, "to give my real name, but they would have learnt it anyway from my cheque. It certainly made them hurry up quicker than they would have done if I had just been Mr. Bofkins!"

Delisia laughed.

"You don't look like Mr. Bofkins! Incidentally that reminds me I don't know the Christian name of my uncle."

"That was certainly a slip, Delisia. I have a variety of names, but I am usually known as 'Rex'. So to you I am 'Uncle Rex'. But I think it would be a mistake for you to call yourself 'Delisia'."

"Yes, of course, my Lord, I thought of that. If Papa heard you had someone called Delisia aboard your yacht, it would be fatal."

"I agree. So tell me what I should call you."

"I think that 'Delia' would be safe and as it is part of my name, I will not forget it."

"Very well, 'Delia' it is – it is a strange name, but then everything about today has been strange and certainly something I never expected in my wildest dreams."

"You have been so wonderful to me," the newly-named Delia sighed, "that I do not know how to put into words how grateful I am and how exciting it is for me to be leaving England."

She drew a deep breath before she added,

"I will not feel really safe until there is a lot of sea between me and the Comte."

"Unless he has wings he will not be able to catch us and I gave no instructions in either of my households as to where I was going. I merely told them I was leaving to go abroad and they may assume I am going to Paris, as in fact I often do."

"I can see you are very intelligent," said Delia, "and I have already guessed that you are going to Egypt not just for amusement, but because you have some serious work to undertake there."

"What sort of work do you imagine that I would be likely to do?" the Marquis asked mockingly.

There was silence for a moment before she replied,

"I think you are acting in a diplomatic capacity and perhaps the Prime Minister has sent you on some mission."

The Marquis stared at her.

"How on earth," he exploded, "did you come to that conclusion? Unless you are reading my thoughts."

"Please don't be angry with me, my Lord, but I can read the thoughts of some people and I know whether they are good or bad because I understand exactly what they are thinking.

"The Comte is bad and wicked, and I don't have to read his thoughts to be sure of it. I think you are what you are and that is an English gentleman in the best sense of the word, and you are kind, understanding and sympathetic to those who are in trouble – most of all, you hate cruelty in any form."

The Marquis stared at her.

"How could you possibly know all this?" he asked. "Whether it is true or untrue, it is something I have never heard before from a woman."

Delia gave a little laugh.

"If you go to Egypt, you must believe in your *Third Eye*. Surely you were taught that the Pharaohs always had one in the centre of their foreheads and it told them what to do and what made the Egyptian people follow them."

"Of course I have heard of the *Third Eye*, but I have never been credited with having one."

"But you know that it is there, my Lord, and that is what we will both need to use when we reach Egypt. But you have not yet told me what you are being sent to do and why you need an interpreter to accompany you."

"I will tell you later on, Delia, but at the moment you are really frightening me because you are not the least what I expected. I find it hard to believe this conversation is actually taking place."

"If it upsets you I will be very careful not to speak of it again, but it will be very difficult not to in Egypt, if we have to use our *Third Eyes*."

"Of course I want you to talk about it to me. I am only surprised, in fact astonished, that I am discussing such a subject with a woman, especially one who looks as if she is only fifteen!"

Delia laughed and it was a very pretty sound.

"Anything is better, my Lord, than that you should be bored with me before we have even left the road – now please tell me where we are going."

"We are going directly to my yacht, for the simple reason that I do not want anyone in my house in Park Lane to see you. It is the first place your father will go to if he becomes suspicious that I have taken you away."

Delia gave a little gasp, but the Marquis continued,

"I have always said that servants see more and talk more than most of us expect them to do."

"You are quite right about that and I promise you I will not talk to anyone or say anything you have not told me to say."

The Marquis smiled at her.

"Thank you, Delia, and now I am going to take you to *The Scimitar* where one of my grooms will be waiting to drive the chaise back to my Mews."

Delia was listening intently and he went on,

"I want you to allow me to drop you off a little way along the Embankment so that the groom will have driven away before you actually step onto the yacht. It is already getting dark and, although I hate to leave you alone, I feel quite certain if you walk quickly towards the yacht where I will be waiting for you, you will come to no harm, and our one contact with my London house will already have left."

Delia clasped her hands together.

"You are so clever," she enthused, "and, of course, I will not be frightened. You are quite right not to let any of your servants see me."

Dusk was now approaching fast, although the sun had not yet completely disappeared.

This meant that there were not many people about.

The Marquis left Delia about a hundred yards down the Embankment.

"You can see the yacht from here," he said, "and as soon as you see the horses drive away, you can run to join me."

He felt with her hair falling over her shoulders that she looked just like a child.

It was unlikely that anyone would stop and speak to her, though a man might easily try to approach a grown-up woman.

At the same time he was feeling worried – perhaps he should have thought of some other method to ensure the news would not be carried back to his house in Park Lane.

He dropped Delia off, where to his relief, that part of the Embankment seemed empty of people.

"Don't talk to anyone and walk as fast as you can without overtaking the horses, Delia. If anyone does speak to you, tell them your uncle is just ahead."

"You think of everything, my Lord, and I am not frightened – at least not very much."

The Marquis drew the horses to a standstill.

"You are quite certain you will not disappear into the sky?" she asked him, "and I will find that this is all just a dream!"

"I will be waiting for you at *The Scimitar* and your *Third Eye* should be telling you that I am just as anxious to have you with me as you are to leave England."

She smiled at him and as she climbed down from the chaise, she cried,

"You are wonderful! Wonderful! I am the luckiest girl in the world."

"I hope you will still be able to say that when we come back, Delia."

He did not wait for her answer, but drove on.

To his relief he found his groom waiting just a few yards from where *The Scimitar* was moored and he took the two cases containing Delia's clothes out of the chaise.

"Take the horses back home carefully and slowly," the Marquis ordered the groom. "They have come a good long way and very fast."

"I'll see to them alright, my Lord, and I hopes your Lordship has a good voyage."

"I hope so too, Wilkins. Look after the horses until I get back."

"I'll do that, my Lord."

"Thank you, Wilkins!"

As the Marquis was speaking, he was carrying the cases towards the wall of the Embankment. Beyond it he could see the masts of *The Scimitar*.

He reached the steps leading down to the water's edge – and then as he turned around the chaise was already some distance away and Delia was running towards him.

"Are you really still here?" she asked breathlessly. "I was half afraid that you might be some way down the Thames already."

"That is where we will be in a very short time," the Marquis smiled at her. "Come aboard now and allow me introduce my charming young niece to the Captain of *The Scimitar*."

# CHAPTER THREE

The Captain welcomed the Marquis on-board *The Scimitar* and said how delighted he was to have his niece as a passenger.

They walked into the attractively decorated Saloon and the Marquis realised without her saying anything that Delia appreciated it.

"What we would really like," the Marquis asked the Captain, "is something to eat. We have driven up from the country without stopping and we are both very hungry."

"I will tell the chef immediately, my Lord, and I am sure that he has your Lordship's *pâté* sandwiches ready and that there is a bottle of champagne on ice."

"You think of everything, Captain, and you know I appreciate it."

The Captain smiled and left the Saloon.

"I am glad," said Delia, "you ordered something to eat. I could not eat any breakfast because I was so worried by what Papa had told me. And now I am starving."

The Marquis laughed.

"I am feeling hungry myself and I promise you will not starve. My chef is excellent and you will scarcely be surprised to hear that he is French."

"Then we must be very careful what we say in front of him as I believe there are many more French in Egypt than there are English."

"I will tell you about that later, but now let us enjoy

ourselves and be so thankful that we have escaped without being stopped by your father."

The yacht's engines had begun turning as soon as they had come aboard and Delia was now aware that they were already moving into the middle of the Thames.

"This is really the most exciting adventure that has ever happened to me, my Lord, and thank you, thank you for being so brilliant. At last I feel safe!"

She seemed so thrilled that the Marquis felt as if he had really achieved something remarkable.

He had been rather afraid that somehow at the very last moment Delia would be prevented from accompanying him on his journey.

If she actually spoke Arabic as fluently as she said she did, she would be of enormous assistance to him once he arrived in Cairo.

He felt if he told her exactly what he was trying to discover in Egypt, she might, by the sheer fact of speaking and understanding Arabic, provide him with the answer to the Prime Minister's burning question.

He poured a glass of champagne and held it out to Delia.

To his surprise she shook her head.

"Mama would never allow me to drink alcohol until I was seventeen and then only at Christmas and at special parties when I was allowed just a tiny sip in the bottom of the glass."

The Marquis smiled understandingly and asked,

"In which case what will you prefer to drink?"

"Fresh lemonade if possible or just water. I really do not mind. I have often thought that champagne, which people make so much fuss about, is overrated."

The Marquis chuckled.

*"Out of the mouths of babes and sucklings,"* he then quoted, "one certainly learns the truth but thank you, Delia, for being so sensible."

He was surprised that she should be so perceptive about the champagne, but he knew that she was right.

She looked very young with her lovely golden hair cascading down either side of her face.

In the plain white gown she had been wearing ever since leaving the shop and which he was sure was just the right dress for a girl of fifteen to wear, she looked ethereal.

"I will leave you alone for a moment, Delia, while I talk to my valet. As I told you, he will be the only one on board who will know the truth of who you are. I want to catch him before he is told by the crew that I have brought my niece aboard with me. He might inadvertently say I do not possess one."

That, in fact, was somewhat unlikely.

Hutton had been with him on many secret missions and he never opened his mouth without thinking of what he was saying – in most cases asking the Marquis first.

*The Scimitar*, which the Marquis was inordinately proud of, had not only been constructed to his own plans, but he had furnished it himself.

For his cabin he had even brought in a four-poster bed that everyone thought was more suited to his ancestral home than a yacht, but it was, as the Marquis pointed out, far more comfortable than the usual bed fitted in a yacht.

The same applied to all the other cabins where there were bunks that were nearly double the width of normal beds and each cabin was draped with curtains as if it was in a private house.

The Marquis supervised the cabin furniture himself and made sure that every woman had enough drawers and hanging-space for her clothes.

He had supposed that he would be regularly taking some lovely woman with him on his travels and she would expect to be made as comfortable as if in his home.

He had, however, found, as many had before, that women at sea were a tiresome nuisance – they were either seasick or demanding to go shopping at every port!

If there happened to be more than one woman on-board, they would invariably end up by fighting with each other, either over the man who had invited them aboard or simply out of jealousy on some other account.

The Marquis had at first tried holding two or three small house parties aboard his yacht, because he wanted to show it off when it was finished.

He decided that each one had been, if not a disaster, at least a bore.

He had then invited alone, one of his beauties who he was having an *affaire-de-coeur* with whilst her husband was in America, but she too had bored him long before *The Scimitar* had turned for home.

It was then that he vowed that in future he would either travel alone or in the company of just one other man whose conversation interested him.

What he actually preferred, he finally decided, was being alone.

He liked to spend as much time as possible on the bridge with the Captain whom he found a most interesting man, quite apart from his naval experience.

Being at sea also gave him time to read, as when he was at home, he always found there was too much to see to and too much to do.

It was inevitable therefore that he fell behind with his reading.

All the new books that were really interesting were delivered automatically by his bookseller in Piccadilly, and he found nothing more enjoyable when at sea than lying in his large four-poster and reading a good book.

He had had so many adventures himself, especially when he was in India and he therefore found the stories of others with more or less the same experiences fascinating.

India had taught him to be always on guard and not to take anything for granted.

Although the average sightseer was not aware of it, there was invariably a spy peeping around every corner – spying out the land for the Russian Czar and sending secret reports back to St. Petersburg.

If he was to be in any way useful in Egypt, he knew that he must be always on the alert and it would certainly be of enormous help if Delia was really as fluent in Arabic as she claimed.

Equally he realised that by helping her to escape he was jeopardising his own future.

As he had told Delia, if it became known that she, a *debutante* of eighteen had travelled alone with him on his yacht, her reputation would be completely ruined.

And he would be forced to marry her.

'I must be very very careful,' he told himself.

But he recognised that there was only one person who could really help him –

One person who would be, in fact, a watchdog over the two of them and that was Hutton!

Hutton was getting on for forty.

He was a small and dark-haired man for whom the Marquis had a great respect and he had been in many tight corners with him, but never once had he lost his composure or become in any way hysterical or even afraid.

In addition he had been instrumental in saving his Master's life on at least two occasions.

"They ought to give you a medal for what you have done," the Marquis had praised Hutton.

"It'd only be a nuisance, my Lord," he had replied, "People'd want to know why I'd won it, and you knows as well as I do that it is the least said the better, where we be concerned."

The Marquis knew this to be true.

"Keep any medals and everythin' else till I retires," Hutton had blustered. "Then, my Lord, you can put 'em in the grave with me and where I goes I 'opes there'll be no nosey-parkers pokin' round to see why I won it!"

The Marquis had laughed as it was impossible to do anything else.

But when Hutton did save his life, he then refused to take any credit for it and what was more, he would not allow the Marquis to increase his salary.

"What you and I does together, my Lord, be our own business, and what you gives me is all I requires at the moment. Perhaps when I'm in a wheelchair, I'll ask you to pay for someone to push it!"

It was just the sort of answer that Hutton made to everything in life.

The Marquis often considered that he enjoyed being with Hutton on his trips more than with anyone else.

*

He now found Hutton in his cabin and the door to the cabin allotted to Delia was open.

He knew that Hutton would look in surprise at the contents of the suitcases they had brought with them from the shop, so he walked into his own cabin and closed the door behind him.

Hutton, who was hanging clothes up in a cupboard, turned round.

"Evenin', my Lord, you was here much quicker that I 'spected, thinkin' you'd have to listen to a lot of that talk at The Priory."

"I didn't stay as long as I intended, Hutton, because I had to visit Lord Durham. When I was there, I found that he was ill-treating his daughter in a way that shocked me considerably."

"It don't surprise me a bit. His Lordship overrides and be 'orribly rough with his 'orses, beatin' 'em at times unmercifully."

"You never told me about that before, Hutton!" the Marquis exclaimed.

"What were the point? Your Lordship has enough troubles of your own without worryin' about him."

The Marquis was quiet for a while and then he said,

"He was not beating his horses when I went to call on him, but threatening to thrash his daughter if she did not marry a man she utterly disliked."

Hutton was listening although he did not speak.

"As you may have guessed, Hutton, when she ran away from her father and the man he was compelling her to marry, she begged for my help. So I have brought her on board with me."

"It be strange after all your Lordship has said, that we should have female company," Hutton remarked. "But I suppose your Lordship knows what you're a-doin'."

"Of course I do, and if it is ever discovered, I will be obliged to marry her. I am looking to you, Hutton, to save me as you have done in the past. You must make sure that everyone on *The Scimitar*, especially the Captain and the crew, all believe her to be my niece."

He saw Hutton was turning this over in his mind.

"I don't suppose anyone aboard has been lookin' at

your Lordship's family tree. But what about them as we'll meet when we gets to Egypt?"

"It has been worrying me even before I went to see Lord Durham, as I had already asked the Prime Minister to find an interpreter for me in Arabic and he said they were difficult to find."

He paused and could see that Hutton was listening although he made no comment.

"What I discovered when Miss Delia asked for my help was that she speaks fluent Arabic."

Hutton's eyes lit up.

"Well, that's somethin' your Lordship'll definitely find useful and you can bet your very last shillin' that them Gippies, like all those other natives never say to you what they be thinkin'."

"I know, Hutton, and I believe Miss Delia will be most useful to us. She is, however, pretending to be only fifteen, and you must make quite certain that no one thinks for a moment that she is any older – "

Hutton said nothing and the Marquis knew he was thinking that it would be impossible to disguise as a young girl a woman who was old enough to be married.

He thought that Hutton would have a surprise when he saw Delia.

He therefore commented,

"She will be in her cabin shortly and I am sure that when you have unpacked for her, you will see that we have bought exactly the right clothes for a girl of that age. You may find it difficult yourself to think that she is any older."

"I just 'opes, my Lord, that Arabic be as clear to her as it ain't to your Lordship or to me. She may well be a blessin' in disguise."

"That is what I believe her to be and she is indeed in

disguise. I am relying on you, Hutton, as I always have, to make sure that no one is suspicious about her."

"Leave it to me, my Lord, and I just 'ope we're not putting our 'eads into nooses!"

"I hope so too," the Marquis agreed heartily.

He washed his hands in the bathroom which opened out of his cabin.

Then he left the cabin intending to go on deck.

As he passed the cabin that Delia was to use he saw she was already opening the cases they had brought from the shop.

"I have instructed my valet, Hutton, to unpack for you, Delia, but as you are here, I want you to meet him."

"Of course, my Lord, and this is such a delightful cabin. I do think you have decorated it beautifully and I am thrilled there is so much room for my clothes."

That was just the sort of praise the Marquis liked to hear, so he smiled at Delia before responding,

"I have learnt, and it was indeed a hard lesson, that all women need plenty of drawer and hanging space and I see you are no exception."

"I am really thrilled with my new clothes, my Lord, and I have not really said thank you to you for them."

"You will thank me by wearing them, Delia, and if you are thinking of changing for dinner, the answer is no, because dinner is now ready. As I have already said, I am famished."

He put out his hand.

"Come and meet Hutton. He is such an important person in my life and I am sure he will be in yours too."

He took her into the Master cabin.

Hutton rose as they entered.

"I found Miss Delia in her cabin, Hutton, so I have brought her in to meet you. I told her you will maid her far better than any lady's maid or nanny she has ever had!"

Delia held out her hand.

"His Lordship was saying so many flattering things about you, Hutton, that I was almost afraid that I might be disappointed!"

Hutton laughed – it was the sort of remark he really enjoyed.

"We'll just have to wait and see, Miss Delia, and I can only congratulate his Lordship on havin' found you."

"I think as a matter of fact," Delia answered him, "*I* found him, but he has been so kind and understanding and I am very very happy to be on-board this lovely yacht."

"Which, thank Heavens, boasts a good chef," the Marquis interrupted. "And I am longing for my dinner."

"So am I," agreed Delia.

As she turned towards the door, she smiled again at Hutton.

"His Lordship says that you will kindly unpack my clothes. Thank you very much. I am so glad not to have to do it myself."

"You leave 'em all to me, miss, and you'll have no need to worry about 'em again."

The Marquis was already past the door and walking towards the companionway.

Delia ran after him and slipped her hand into his.

"He is so like a character from a book," she said in a whisper. "How could you be lucky enough to have found anyone like him?"

"Hutton has been with me for many years. He is more amusing and reliable than anyone I have ever met."

"I think that is the nicest compliment you could pay anyone and I should feel honoured if you said it about me."

"I will let you know if you deserve it at the end of the journey," the Marquis laughed.

"I will be waiting, but I can see you are intending to be very critical."

"Of course I am," the Marquis retorted. "You have to pay for your passage by proving you are as efficient as you have told me you are!"

It was impossible for Delia to answer him as they had by now reached the Saloon.

Two Stewards were waiting to serve dinner.

The Marquis sat down at the top of the table and he indicated to Delia to sit on his right.

Before the first course could be served, the Marquis whispered to her,

"Now you must remember, Delia, that from now on in front of the servants you are to call me 'Uncle Rex'."

The first course was delicious and was followed by two further courses that only a superb French chef could have concocted.

Finally after coffee and the Marquis had accepted a liqueur, the Stewards withdrew.

When the door was closed Delia sighed,

"Now I do feel much better. I was so hungry I was beginning to think I might float away and you would have to manage the rest of your journey without an interpreter!"

"I realised we were both hungry, Delia, but to have stopped at any of the inns that we passed would have been playing directly into your father's hands. We would have been exposed if he enquired as to whether there had been a customer with four magnificent stallions and a very pretty young woman with him."

"I realised that, my Lord, and that is why I did not complain, but I was far too agitated this morning to eat any breakfast and dinner last night seems a long way away."

The Marquis laughed.

"If you are still hungry, I will tell Hutton to leave some biscuits by your bed, so that you can gobble them up at night."

"How could I be hungry after that delicious dinner, but I will surely grow very fat if every meal on this voyage is equally tempting. To send away any dish would insult your chef."

"If there is one thing I dislike," said the Marquis, "it is bad food. Half the pleasure of being at sea, unless you are seasick, is to really enjoy the meals. That is why I employ this particular French chef"

"I will go and talk to him and practise my French, although I am very fluent. Of course, the majority of the girls at my school were French."

"It is certainly my good fortune that you shared a room with an Egyptian girl, Delia, and now I will tell you briefly why we will go ashore at Alexandria and then on to Cairo."

"I am listening intently, my Lord, and I think from what you have already told me that the British are not only curious about the Suez Canal but are regretting they did not take a large share in it."

The Marquis stared wide-eyed at her.

"I definitely did not tell you that was the reason as to why I am making this voyage!"

"No, you did not tell me, but I reasoned it out for myself, that you would not have left in such a hurry unless you had been sent on a specific mission. That meant that either the Prime Minister himself or the Secretary of State for Foreign Affairs had asked for your help."

The Marquis could hardly believe what he was now hearing.

"At my school the French girls were always talking about the Suez Canal," Delia went on, "boasting about how clever they had been to promote it, while the British had been against the whole idea from the very beginning."

The Marquis was astonished.

"Just how could you have possibly thought all that out for yourself?"

"It was not really all that difficult. The French girls kept saying how excited their fathers were about the Canal. The Egyptian girl I shared with told me what rows there had been because slaves had been employed to build it."

She paused for a moment and then continued,

"Some fathers of the pupils had invested money in the Suez Canal project and were frightened that the British would force them to lose it."

As she spoke the Marquis remembered that 'in the cause of humanity and justice' the British Government had protested against the use of slave labour – it had only been discontinued finally by their threatening to stop it by force.

It was the French who supported de Lesseps when he had turned to the Emperor Louis Napoleon for help and investment, and thanks to him the work had steamed ahead swiftly through the use of dredgers and rock-busters.

The labourers were no longer slaves, but a motley collection of different nationalities attracted by a wage of over a shilling a day.

He recalled hearing the new workers were called 'a Babel of Nations' and it was they who were responsible for Ismail receiving from the Turkish Sultan in 1867 his new title of Khedive instead of Viceroy.

It was little wonder that he was now, as the Prime Minister had said, inviting all the European Heads of State to the Grand Opening, which was to take place next March.

The Marquis had been wondering just how he was going explain this complicated position to a young girl.

Yet Delia knew as much about it as he did himself!

"You surprise me," he now said aloud. "I thought I should have to start at the very beginning and tell you why the Suez Canal has always been a dream of Ferdinand de Lesseps."

"There is much more I want to know, my Lord, and please forgive me if I seem stupid over many matters, but I do know a bit about the Suez Canal because I was at school in France."

"I think as it happens, Delia, you know a great deal more than I do. Therefore we must exchange information so we do not make the mistake of leaving one or the other ignorant as events unfold."

"You need not be afraid of that. After all we will be together and I will know instinctively when you want me to listen intently, or perhaps to ask awkward questions in the same way as a French girl might."

"I have come to the conclusion that you are a most intelligent girl. In fact, I think you are unique, for I am quite convinced that the average girl of your age knows very little about anything except how to dance, and how, if possible, to attract the nearest young man."

Now he was speaking with a cynical note creeping into his voice.

Delia did not answer.

"What are you thinking?" he asked abruptly.

"I was just thinking," Delia replied quietly, "that it is unnecessary for you to be upset by and afraid of women."

The Marquis stared at her.

"Why should you deduce that I am either of those things?"

"Because you told me you were running away from a woman and I have heard you say scathing and somewhat bitter words against women."

She sighed and then continued softly,

"Not all women are like you think they are and if that is what you have experienced, it is because you are too good-looking and possess an important title."

The Marquis did not argue, he just looked at her.

Then she went on,

"One day you will find someone who suits you and who will really love you just for yourself. But because you have so far failed to meet such a woman, it is really a great mistake to think that they are all the same and to treat them as enemies."

The Marquis felt he could not be hearing her aright.

How was it possible that this young slip of a girl, who looked as if she was still at school could speak to him in a way he might have expected from his grandmother?

"You astound me!" he exclaimed.

"I am so sorry. You must forgive me if I say what is in my mind. It was the way I was able to talk to Mama when she was alive. Since then there has been no one in my life intelligent enough to understand what I am trying to say."

"And you think that is what I am?"

"Forgive me, my Lord, I should not – have spoken to you so frankly. I see now it was a wrong thing for me to do and presuming inexcusably on our short acquaintance."

She was so contrite that the Marquis was obliged to reply,

"You are not to apologise and, of course, you are to talk to me about any subject that interests you and I will enjoy listening. It is just that I am finding it surprising that on such a very short acquaintance you should understand so much about me."

"It was Mama who taught me to study people in the same way I would study a book. It is what I did at school, especially when new girls or new mistresses arrived.

"I soon found out that in nine cases out of ten I was absolutely right about them, although naturally I did not say aloud all that was going through my mind."

The Marquis hesitated and she added quickly,

"I am sorry, it was rude and very foolish of me and I will not do so again."

"But, of course, you must do it again," the Marquis assured her. "If we are to work together, we must always be absolutely frank with each other. It was just that I was astonished at you being so observant or maybe I should say so perceptive. Although my instinct is to argue and claim you are wrong, I really cannot truthfully do so."

Delia laughed.

"Now you are being very kind and perhaps a little condescending. As I have already said, it was very foolish of me to say just what was in my mind, but I think it was because it is so exciting to be on this amazing adventure with you – and I was jumping my fences too quickly."

"From what you have just said, I imagine that you are a keen horsewoman and do you talk to your horses as you talk to me?"

The Marquis was clearly making a joke of it, but Delia answered him seriously,

"I adore riding and naturally I should have asked you to tell me about your horses before I started talking to you about yourself. Yes, I have always believed that one should talk to one's horse, especially when you are getting to know him and want him to obey you."

The Marquis believed that this sort of instruction was only given to advanced pupils and it was known to all experienced riders like himself.

Because he knew it would please Delia, he said,

"I always talk to my horse before I enter him into a big race and especially if I want him to jump exceptionally high jumps."

Delia smiled.

"I am sure and, of course, we must talk more about our horses."

"The one thing I am certain of, Delia, is that I find this conversation quite extraordinary. We will have plenty of time to get to know each other on this voyage and also to discuss every move we make before we make it."

As he spoke he realised that this was something he had never before said to anyone, except perhaps to Hutton.

*Least of all to a woman.*

In fact, now he came to think about it, he had never held a serious conversation with any woman as they were always talking about themselves or flattering him.

He glanced at Delia in the candlelight and thought how lovely and yet how childlike she was.

"You were speaking earlier about your *Third Eye*," he said. "Do you think you are using it when you study all the people around you, and is it possible, as the Egyptians believe, that we all really do have one?"

"Of course we do, but everyone needs to develop it. You might call it perception or sensitivity, or anything you like, but actually it is the *Third Eye* that makes our lives either a success or a failure.

"In our contact with people it shows us very clearly whether they are truthful or lying, friend or foe."

"And you have found that in your own short life?" the Marquis asked incredulously.

"You are really asking me what I *really* believe in," replied Delia. "Of course, the majority of the people in the East believe in the '*Wheel of Rebirth*' – as I do."

The Marquis knew it was hopeless to ask her how she could know and understand such an esoteric subject.

She was a phenomenon and so completely different from anyone he had ever met.

He therefore enquired quite simply,

"Tell me why that is what you believe in and what evidence you have that it really exists."

"You question the concept because it comes from the East, but all the Eastern races believe that they have innumerable lives to live, each successive one depending on their behaviour in their preceding life, being better or worse than they have achieved before."

The Marquis himself had actually studied the *Wheel of Rebirth* or reincarnation as an undergraduate at Oxford and he had often discussed the subject with several elderly sages who had spent much of their lives in the East.

Then he had paid scant attention, but now he was becoming interested.

"Are you actually telling me, Delia, that perhaps in your last incarnation you were Egyptian, which is why you can now speak the language so fluently?"

"It is certainly a possibility but I think perhaps I did not advance as far as I should have, and I have therefore come back in this life to a great number of difficulties that I could have well avoided if indeed I had done better in my previous incarnation."

The Marquis chuckled.

"It sounds to me much like school."

"Why should it be anything else?" she asked. "All I do know is that I have my *Third Eye* and you could call it an innate perception about people and events. *I am never mistaken.*"

The Marquis raised his eyebrows, but Delia carried on,

"It is a talent I can only have acquired from another life, because my present father has no instinct whatsoever, while my mother, from whom I must have inherited it, was always aware of whether people were good or bad."

"Now you are telling me something I can accept."

She saw there was a rather scornful look on his face and added quickly,

"Of course that is only a small part of the belief that activates hundreds of thousands of people in every part of the world – "

Her voice softened as she persevered,

"For all those who worship at Mecca or live in the heights of Nepal or the plains of India, it is a reality which pushes them to strive fervently so that when they leave this life they will be certain to secure a more desirable situation and personality in their next one."

"I know that this was a belief held by Buddha," the Marquis remarked. "But it is something I have not heard discussed much in England and I am only astonished that you are saying all this to me now."

"I am sorry if I have surprised you, my Lord, but I recognised as soon as I saw you that you were so different from the average man Papa entertains."

There was a short silence and then she blurted out almost dramatically,

"I know that you have undertaken some outstanding

deeds either in this life or a previous one and it has left its mark on you!"

"How on earth can you say that, Delia?"

"I just know it to be true and I am certain that when you have been very close to death and saved yourself only by a hair's breadth, you thought that you must live because there were still many more things for you to do in this life, important not just to yourself but to all those who trust and rely on you."

The Marquis sat back in his chair.

"I just don't believe that this conversation is taking place. With your hair falling down on each side of your face you do not look even fifteen, yet you are talking to me as if you were a Professor at a University or perhaps one of the Holy men I encountered in India."

"I wish it was true," laughed Delia. "But I am sure, although you do not like to talk about it, that you know you have a special mission to perform in this life."

She could see that the Marquis was listening to her intensely and she continued,

"The mission may have already happened and you would know when it did. Or if it is still to come, you will suddenly become aware of what is expected of you, if you are not aware of it already."

The Marquis thought back.

It was in fact his intuition which had enabled him to save that small British garrison in India from destruction – and to prevent what might have turned out to be a disaster.

It was a traumatic event in his life that he had never talked about to anyone.

Yet he had definitely foreseen what was likely to occur and forestalled it, simply because he was convinced of what was about to happen.

He had often thought afterwards that any other man might have walked away from the fort, because it was none of his business, or perhaps because he was only imagining the danger and had no actual proof of it.

Now in some extraordinary way this child, because she seemed to be nothing else, was telling him that it was an event that had been preordained in his life – what he had dismissed as pure instinct was very real and had been given to him by a Power greater than himself.

While he was thinking he had not spoken, but Delia had been watching him.

Now she rose to her feet.

"I think as we are both tired, we should go to bed," she suggested. "I can only thank you once again for your wonderful kindness in rescuing me from a terrible fate and bringing me here with you."

She smiled before she added,

"I think I must have known when I climbed into the box at the back of your chaise that you were as you are, and not as you might have been – "

Before the Marquis could reply, she had walked to the door.

Then as he somewhat belatedly rose to his feet, she went out closing the door behind her.

He heard her running down the companionway.

He sat down again in his seat at the table.

'I really don't believe this is happening to me,' he thought. 'It is incredible and I must be dreaming.'

# CHAPTER FOUR

The crew were delighted with Delia.

The Marquis had chosen older men to be his crew as there were intervals when he did not take his yacht to sea.

He thought young men could find the work boring and get into trouble, and so he therefore preferred men who were over thirty-five and as the crew had already been with him a few years many of them were even older.

From the moment she appeared they took what the Marquis considered was a fatherly interest in Delia.

They treated her as a child and he could not help his eyes twinkling when the chef one day made her a chocolate ice cream in the form of a bear sitting upright in a pool of strawberry jelly.

She had gone to the galley and talked to the chef in French, so that every day he tried to think of a new dish to entertain the child.

Although Delia was not a child, she was certainly amused and delighted by all this attention.

"See how kind he is," she said to the Marquis when her pudding appeared as a swan sailing on rippling waves. "He spoils me and I love every minute of it!"

She enjoyed her favourite dishes and when the chef thought that his Lordship might become bored with them, he served a different dish for each of them.

She certainly seemed to enjoy his yacht more than any other woman he had ever known.

She was up early in the morning running around on deck even before he appeared.

The Captain, which was certainly unusual, enjoyed having her on the bridge with him.

She was absolutely thrilled when they arrived at the Port of Gibraltar.

She found all the shops enchanting, but unlike other women did not ask for endless expensive presents.

She only asked the Marquis if he would buy her a few ribbons for her hair and when she wore a bow of blue ribbon just above each eye, it made her look even younger than ever.

The Marquis did not want to stay long in Gibraltar.

But the yacht had to take on extra stores and fuel at Malta and Valetta was another opportunity for Delia to go ashore.

They visited various shops, buying some items the Marquis wanted including books.

When they returned to *The Scimitar*, it was to find a man seated cross-legged on the deck – he had on show a large amount of jewellery in antique settings that Delia had never seen before.

She stood still gazing at them and the man said to the Marquis,

"This is an amazing opportunity, my Lord. These beautiful and expensive jewels were left me by a lady who is now dead. I have to sell them because my wife is ill and my children are hungry."

The Marquis thought he had heard that story before.

But the jewellery was certainly very attractive.

He picked up a brooch set in a way which had been fashionable a hundred years earlier.

"That is one of my very best pieces, my Lord," the man blustered, "and I'll let you have it for – "

He paused a moment, then named an amount in the local Maltese currency that the Marquis calculated at five hundred pounds.

He hesitated, thinking it was quite a lot of money to pay when at the moment he had no one to give the brooch to.

Then he could see that Delia was looking straight at him with a strange expression in her eyes.

She did not speak and she did not move and yet he knew instinctively that she was telling him not to buy the brooch.

He thought it strange as he had been sure that it was genuine and if it was, then the asking price of five hundred pounds was definitely cheap.

Once again he looked at Delia.

He realised that she was telling him without words that it was not what he thought it to be, but a *fake*.

"I tell you what I'll do," he said aloud. "I will buy this brooch from you, but I would like to take it first to a jeweller's shop in Valetta where I have bought jewellery before and where the owner is most obliging – "

He paused, but the man did not speak.

"He is the most respected jeweller in Malta and he will tell me if I am getting the bargain from you which you tell me I am."

He hesitated and looked round before he added,

"You can of course come with me and wait outside while I speak to him."

He put the brooch back with the other jewels that were spread out on a cloth on the deck.

Then he turned to Delia,

"Come and help me to find my chequebook which I think I have left on the writing table in my cabin. As the sun is shining and it is very hot, you had better bring a hat if you are accompanying me."

He walked across the deck as he spoke and Delia followed him through the door that led to the Saloon.

When they on their own, the Marquis asked her,

"Why did you tell me that the brooch is not what he says it is?"

Delia smiled.

"So you understood I was willing you to realise it is a fake?"

"How can you know that, Delia? It looks genuine enough to me and, if it is, I would be buying a bargain."

"So you would, my Lord, but whilst the setting is genuine – the diamonds are not."

"How can you be so sure?"

He was thinking that Delia was rather showing off and pretending to be knowledgeable about diamonds which she really could not be and without even closely inspecting them.

"I suppose that you will think it stupid of me to say I was using my *Third Eye*."

"I do not believe a *Third Eye* or any other eye could possibly say if that diamond brooch is genuine or not, and anyway we will very soon know if our plausible salesman allows me to show it to an expert."

As he spoke he left the Saloon and opened the door onto the deck and then he laughed.

"All right, Delia," he called out, "*you win!*"

She joined the Marquis and then looked towards the

place on the deck where the salesman had been sitting with his wares.

The space was empty and he had gone.

"I can see that you are extremely valuable," said the Marquis, "in more ways than one. I must be grateful and say thank you for saving me from wasting my money."

"You will have to be careful of men like him, my Lord. They are to be found all over the place in Paris and I suppose in other big Cities."

The Marquis thought, as he had thought before, that was the sort of warning he should be giving *her*!

He realised that she had not needed to be an expert on diamonds. It was her *Third Eye* which had told her that the man was a rogue.

Hers undoubtedly was a very special gift that most people would appreciate and find very useful.

They went ashore again, but there was no sign of the dishonest jewel-seller.

There were, however, very many beggars and other people trying to sell souvenirs.

"I must give you a present," the Marquis suggested, as they walked into a street filled with expensive shops.

"No, of course not, my Lord," Delia responded.

The Marquis looked at her in surprise.

"Why ever not?"

"Because you have given me so much already and as I have no money with me, there is nothing I can give you in return."

"If you want money, Delia, you know only too well I will give you all you want."

"But if I buy you a gift and you are really paying for it, it would not be the sort of gift I should want to give you.

One day, although it may take a long time, I will give you something I know you will appreciate and which in a small way will tell you how grateful I am to you."

The Marquis smiled.

"Very well, I will wait, and I am quite certain I will be most delighted with any present you might give me, but I have every intention of giving you one now, so you had better tell me what you would like."

They were passing a shop with a number of pretty dresses in the window.

One particular evening dress was of soft lace and it was particularly attractive as the pattern of the lace was a flower design and in the middle of each flower was a small diamante.

The Marquis, gazing at it, had to admit that it was one of the prettiest gowns he had ever seen.

He sensed that Delia loved the dress.

"It is too expensive, I know it is too expensive," she murmured, "but I would like to look pretty for you when we dine together. If the dress is not that outrageously dear, perhaps you could afford it – "

The Marquis became pensive.

When he considered the many expensive gifts he had given to the women with whom he had had *affaires-de-coeur*, he knew the cost of this particular gown would in comparison seem insignificant.

They entered the shop.

And when Delia put on the gown the Marquis knew it did not need her *Third Eye* to tell her it might have been designed especially for her.

It not only fitted her perfectly, but revealed the soft curves of her body and at the same time it shone when the diamante caught the light.

It made her look as if she was dressed in stars rather than in lace.

The Marquis bought it for her.

In addition he insisted on buying her a very smart and up-to-date afternoon gown.

She told him there was no need to buy it, as he had already bought her sufficient clothes at the shop they had patronised in the suburbs of London.

"I have every intention of calling on acquaintances in Cairo, who would expect you, as my niece, to be smartly dressed. I just cannot allow you to let the family down!"

Delia giggled.

"You are only saying that to put me at my ease. Of course I would love the beautiful dress, but I do not wish to impose on you."

"You can easily repay me when I make you work exceedingly hard a little later on – "

She knew he was referring to her understanding of Arabic and so she therefore remained silent when he added a rather cheeky hat the vendeuse informed them went with the dress.

He also provided her with a velvet cape in case they went out in the evening

The vendeuse promised faithfully to deliver all their purchases directly to the yacht.

The Marquis and Delia explored the City of Valetta a little longer, taking coffee seated outside a coffee shop on the pavement.

Delia was thrilled at watching the people pass by.

"I used to long, when I was at my school, to stop at a place like this," she enthused, "and watch the people, but, naturally we were not allowed to."

"Why did you want to watch them, Delia?"

"Because the people of each nationality are so very different – in the way they walk, the way they carry their heads and the way they think."

"Are you now telling me," the Marquis quizzed her, "that you can tell what they are thinking as they pass by?"

"I expect it is only my imagination, but just look at that man walking across the road now and frowning as he does so. He is not worrying at all about the traffic, he is worrying about something that is dramatically affecting his life."

He glanced at the man she was talking about.

"Perhaps he is thinking of taking on an entirely new job," she continued, "which is different from anything he has done before. Or he is upset because the alterations to his house have cost more than he expected."

The Marquis laughed.

"You are making it all up. At the same time it is an excellent way of learning or thinking you are learning more about the people you come into contact with."

Delia was still watching the people passing by.

"Look at that beggar," she cried. "He has just made a nuisance of himself to the man walking down the other side of the street. I think simply because he was a nuisance the man has given him some money."

The Marquis followed the direction of her eyes and saw who she was watching.

The man who had tipped the beggar was moving on quickly, obviously extremely glad to be rid of the beggar who had pestered him.

Then as he disappeared, they saw the beggar hold up the money he had been given. He looked at it and then with a shrug of his shoulders slipped it into his pocket.

Next he looked round for another victim and found a well dressed middle-aged woman coming out of a shop.

"I think by the end of the day," Delia commented wisely, "he will have more in his pocket than you have."

"I wouldn't be surprised. Those beggars are always a nuisance and very persistent. The only way to be rid of them is to pay them off quickly."

"That is just what I was thinking," said Delia, "and perhaps we miss many things in our lives just because we accept far too quickly that it is impossible to obtain what we really want."

The Marquis sipped his coffee.

Then as he searched for a rejoinder to her comment, he realised that he enjoyed these conversations with Delia more than any other discussion he could recall having with anyone else.

He always had to think hard of how to answer her.

She brought to mind situations when he himself had to find rapid answers to the same sort of question.

When they returned to *The Scimitar*, the dresses the Marquis had bought for Delia had already arrived.

Hutton had taken them down to her cabin.

"I am thrilled with all you have given me, my Lord, but I am still upset that I could not buy something for you. I only hope that one day, although it may be very far away, I will find a gift you really want and then I will no longer feel guilty."

"There is no need for you to feel guilty now," the Marquis insisted. "And just remember you saved me from throwing away five hundred pounds this morning!"

"Yes, that is satisfactory at any rate, but actually it would have been very silly of you to spend so much money with a man who did not do enough business to rent a shop, and was thus unlikely to have anything worth buying."

"You are quite right, Delia, and I see I will have to take you with me wherever I go so as to be certain I am not deceived by rogues or make a fool of myself."

"I am certain, even if I had not been there, that you would have applied exactly the same test as you did, and no one could have moved faster than that man did!"

"Well, I have proved one thing to my satisfaction," sighed the Marquis, "and that is that you are protecting me rather more than I am protecting you!"

"I really think," Delia remarked as if she definitely intended to have the last word, "I should try to protect you from myself. You are giving me too much and I cannot see how I can ever pay you back."

The Marquis thought with a twist to his lips that he had never yet been paid back by a woman on whom he had spent a great deal of money.

They had always taken it as their right.

He had reckoned that even before he made love to them they were already asking themselves how generous he would be.

Invariably they would always accept more than he really wished to spend.

'It is not that I am mean,' he had often thought to himself, 'it is just that I dislike the idea of women thinking that, because I am rich, they are therefore entitled to every pound they can squeeze out of me.'

He found it touching that Delia was so different.

She was worrying because she could not give him anything in return.

'I just do not believe that when she grows older,' he thought, 'she will be like the rest, grabbing everything she can lay her hands on and being interested in a man because of his possessions rather than who he is.'

*

As they left Malta, Delia asked where they would be stopping next.

"There is no need for us to stop anywhere before Alexandria," the Marquis replied. "But I suppose you will be disappointed if you do not see Naples or even Greece?"

"You know I would love to see both of them, but if you are in a hurry to reach Egypt and the Suez Canal, we could perhaps stop there on our way back."

It flashed through his mind that she would be in no rush to return home to England, because then would come the dreadful decision as to where she should go and what she should do.

"I think," he said, "that perhaps we could make just one stop on the way. So we will toss for it and let the fates decide for us rather than ourselves."

He could guess without being told which of the two places would appeal most to Delia.

As he flung the coin up into the air, he had the idea that she was praying.

"Heads it is Greece – and tails it is Naples."

The coin fell to the ground between them.

Delia gave a cry of delight.

"It is Greece!" she cried. "I want to go there more than I have ever wanted to go anywhere. I was so afraid you would think it much too far out of our way."

"Your wish has come true, Delia, and I only hope you will not be disappointed."

"How could I be? I have read so many books about Greece and what I would love to see more than anything else is Delphi."

The Marquis considered this for a moment and then he remarked,

"We shall have to sail to Athens first and then have quite a long journey overland to Delphi."

"Can we really do that?"

Her eyes were shining and she looked so lovely that the Marquis thought it would be a very hard-hearted man who would be able to refuse her.

"Very well, Delia, you have successfully bullied me into spending more time on reaching my objective than I intended, but as it is so excellent for your education, I can claim it is in a good cause."

"It is the most perfect and wonderful present I have ever had. I know it will be something to think about and dream about for the rest of my life."

"How do you know you will not come here again?"

Delia did not answer.

After a moment the Marquis commented,

"You know as well as I do, Delia, you will have to marry someone sooner or later and let me suggest that you are not too difficult about it."

"What do you mean 'too difficult'?"

"I would admit that the man your father chose for you sounds totally ghastly and I can quite understand your refusing to marry him, but the perfect man you have seen in your dreams or read about in novels very likely does not exist. Therefore you will have to accept whomever God sends you and not be too fussy."

"And what then are you doing about *your* life?" she asked him unexpectedly. "You said you have no wish to marry anyone but I am certain that your family has told you frequently that you must marry and produce an heir to carry on your title and estates."

The Marquis looked at her in surprise.

Somehow he had not expected Delia to realise that

this was indeed his situation – that it was his duty to have an heir, as his relatives had insisted over and over again.

"There is plenty of time for that," he said sharply. "And as I have already told you, I have no intention at all of marrying someone who I will become bored with and who will make my life a misery."

"But there so many charming women in the world and although you are putting up a barrier between yourself and them, one day someone will be able to sneak through it and you will be really happy."

"Are you saying I am not really happy at present?"

"Only you can answer that question, my Lord, but if you are a really happy man, I don't think you would have planned to set out on this journey alone."

"The trouble with you," the Marquis protested, "is that you are far too occupied using that peculiarity you call your *Third Eye*. I am living my life as I wish to live it and not looking too far forward and certainly not looking back! Does *that* satisfy you?"

Delia sighed.

"It is satisfying to me that you are so kind and so understanding. It is just that, as you make other people happy, I want you to be happy too and, of course, to enjoy all the best things that can never be bought with money."

The Marquis ruminated that once again this strange child was talking sense.

It was indeed an issue he had known himself.

He had lain awake at night wondering what he was doing and where he was going.

"One day you will find the answer," Delia told him.

"You are reading my thoughts again, Delia, and if you continue to do so, I will put up a barrier between us or you will have to stay in your cabin!"

She glanced at the Marquis quizzically to see if he was speaking seriously.

Then she knew he was teasing her.

"I am so sorry, my Lord, you must forgive me if I seem to be impertinent and taking advantage of the unusual situation that we find ourselves in. But it is because you are such an exciting and unusual person that I have to keep watching you and learning so much I did not know before."

The Marquis thought no one could have put it more perceptively or more intelligently.

"Very well, Delia, I forgive you. But no peeping or prying and leave my thoughts to me, please. They are *not* suitable for a girl of your age!"

Delia laughed.

"When you say 'a girl of your age' you are thinking only of this life and the short time I have lived in it. What about all my other lives? If you added them all up, I am sure you would be surprised."

"So once again we are back in that mythical world you believe in, but of which I am somewhat sceptical!"

Delia gave an exaggerated sigh.

"In that case I will have somehow to convince you of the truth before this journey is ended. Otherwise I will have failed those who have sent me to help you."

"And who are they?" the Marquis demanded rather sharply.

Delia made an expressive gesture with her hands.

"How easy it would be if we knew who is directing us, who is saving us from ourselves and who is inspiring us. As even you must admit, we are both inspired to find out more about our present and past lives."

He realised that once again they were embarking on one of those strange yet fascinating conversations in which he found himself striving to find an answer to everything that Delia contended.

Invariably so far, although he was scarcely likely to admit it, she had been far more convincing in her assertions than he in his protestations.

While they were talking, *The Scimitar* had begun to move slowly out of Valetta harbour.

The sun was shining and turning the sea to the deep blue that has inspired poets and writers since the beginning of time.

As if she felt she was missing something, Delia left the Saloon and ran across the deck.

As she looked back at Malta, she thought the island looked very attractive as she reflected that what lay ahead was so exciting she could not put it into words.

She ran to the front of the yacht and now the waves were breaking gently against the bow as the speed of the engines quickened.

It was all *so* beautiful.

It was the movement of the sea, the clouds and the seagulls that was especially thrilling and exhilarating.

As she stood looking ahead the Marquis joined her.

He thought as he did so how smoothly the engines were turning and how *The Scimitar was* living up to all his expectations.

He could see a rapt expression on Delia's face and commented,

"I know just what you are thinking. There is more excitement for you ahead and you are delighted that you are going forward rather than back."

"You are quite right, my Lord, but only you would understand, as other people do not understand, that it is not just a matter of making a voyage, but of seeing and feeling and learning something one has not seen or felt or known before."

The Marquis thought nothing could have expressed more brilliantly exactly what he himself was thinking.

It was, although he just could not put it into words, something different from what in his past had been all too familiar.

Then he asked himself somewhat cynically if it was possible that this young girl could waken him to aspects of life different from anything he had known before.

Yet, although he did not want to admit it, he was thinking of issues that had never previously concerned him.

In a curious way he could understand how much Greece meant to Delia and how she would rather see it than anywhere else in the world.

"You are so right," she murmured. "I have read all about Greece, but no book was ever enough and invariably I was left wanting more."

"What will happen if you are disappointed, Delia?"

"I just don't believe it would ever be possible to be disappointed with Greece. It has been responsible for so much of our modern civilisation and has inspired so many great people."

She spoke with such a rapt note in her voice that, the Marquis thought, it was very touching.

At the same time he could not believe it possible that any young girl could feel so intensely about a country rather than about a man.

After all, he told himself, that was what life was all about – the search for people who meant something to you, rather than the surroundings that, however attractive, were not really personal enough to be of any importance in the long run.

"I know just what you are thinking, my Lord, that I am getting over-excited about Greece and when I see it, I may be disillusioned."

"Yes, that is indeed my thought, Delia, so do not over-excite yourself – please."

Delia laughed.

"You have got it all wrong. Of course I want to see Greece as a place and its wonderful temples. But what I am searching for is what made the Greeks so remarkable at the time. It was not just the beauty of their country or their people."

"Then what would you be looking for?" he asked as she stopped speaking.

"I think that I can only describe it as the spirit of Greece. The spirit that led and inspired them and made them different from any other peoples who have ever lived on this earth."

She drew in her breath and went on slowly,

"Above all they gave us the power of thought – to inspire generations of those who came after them. All that must have come from a Power greater than themselves and which we have been seeking ever since."

She spoke with a catch in her voice that he felt was even more moving than anything she was saying.

She stood looking out at the sea ahead of them and the sunshine glittering on the waves and the Marquis knew that for the moment she had forgotten him and even what she had been saying.

She was inspired by a Power he could not see and could not feel, yet he knew it was there.

Perhaps it was the eternal and everlasting spirit of the Greeks or maybe it was something even more profound and more difficult to find.

*

That evening the chef exceeded himself at dinner with some delicious fruit, fish and spicy ingredients he had found at Malta.

Delia put on the new dress the Marquis had given her.

He had to admit that she looked even lovelier in it than any woman could ever look.

They talked animatedly through the meal arguing with each other in the manner the Marquis was finding so intriguing.

It forced him to come up with an intelligent answer to everything she expounded.

He thought as dinner finished that it had been one of the most demanding meals he had ever enjoyed.

At least a dozen times he found himself searching frantically for a reply to something Delia had said.

He was aware that she was deliberately provoking him, taking an opposite view to almost everything he said.

Several times they had both laughed helplessly at the other's reasoning.

As dinner finished Delia pleaded,

"Please be very kind and send the chef not only our thanks for such a delicious meal but also perhaps a glass of your delicious champagne. You know as well as I do how much a Frenchman enjoys that particular drink, because no one can make it as well as they do."

"You are quite right, Delia, and I certainly should have thought of it."

He called for the Steward and instructed him to take what was left in the bottle of champagne to the chef.

"Ask him to accept it," he said, "as an expression of our gratitude for such an excellent meal."

"Pierre'll like that, my Lord," the Steward replied and carried off the champagne with a grin on his face.

"What shall we do now?" the Marquis asked.

"I noticed when I came aboard, my Lord, that you have a small piano on board, but you have never referred to it, so I thought that perhaps you do not care for music."

"Are you saying you would like to play the piano?"

"Only if you do not mind my doing so. My father for instance has always hated music and the piano at home is pushed away into a sitting room we never use. If anyone suggests music after dinner, he goes to bed."

"I will be very interested to hear what sort of music you can play, Delia, but perhaps I am like your father as I cannot bear amateurs tinkling away at the piano and I did not think that music would be another of your specialities."

"Why ever not?"

"Because on the whole men play better than women and also, as I have said, I like very good music played by professionals, and even then I am not what you might call 'a wild music fan'."

'Fan' was a new word that had only recently come into use and Delia giggled.

"I would like to play just one little piece of music, because I think that it will fit in with the moonlight, but if you feel it is awful, all you have to do is to walk out of the room and go on deck – and then I will join you."

The Marquis thought he had no wish to be rude, but the music he really enjoyed was played by an orchestra and the best musicians.

When such orchestras had played in London he had gone to the Concert Hall alone and had not asked anyone to accompany him.

He knew only too well when a woman was bored,

how she would fidget about, touch her hair or even, as had happened to him more than once, powder her nose because she wished to draw attention to herself, as she resented the music taking his thoughts away from her.

He had found Delia so unusual and amusing and he felt it would be an anti-climax if she played some girlish piece she had learnt at school and he would doubtless find it unmusical and boring.

At the same time because she had suggested it, he supposed he would have to be pleasant about her talent.

However, he now wished he had removed the piano – it had been put there simply because the women he had brought on board had asked if they could dance.

They had wanted his arms round them and they had thought that drifting round the Saloon was far preferable to conversation.

Not only had the music been a failure but so had the parties, and it was then he had decided that when he was on board his yacht, he was far happier alone.

However, he thought it would be somewhat unkind to deny Delia the right to play the piano if that was what she wanted.

He walked to the piano and opened it.

"There is a lot of music tucked down the side, but I expect you have your own."

"Yes, that is so, my Lord."

She pulled out the stool that had been pushed under the piano.

The Marquis walked away to sit down in one of the armchairs.

He thought Delia's back in the sparkling dress he had given her with her shining golden hair cascading over her shoulders was a most beautiful sight.

She had certainly shone tonight even more than she had on other nights.

He recognised that if she was in London, she would undoubtedly be feted as a great beauty within a week.

Yet if they were in London, he would have avoided her at all costs.

He would have much preferred to be monopolised by some married woman like Silvia.

He had never imagined that amongst the *debutantes* there was anyone who could think, talk and look like Delia.

Very very softly Delia was touching the keys.

Now she began to play in a manner that made the Marquis not only listen but stare at her as if he just could not believe his ears.

He had never heard the music she was playing, yet he knew in a way it carried on the conversation they had just finished, which had stimulated his brain so that every word seemed of significance and memorable.

Now her music was doing the same.

It was rousing feelings within him he did not know he even possessed.

It made him listen enraptured whether he wished to or not.

Delia played for about twenty minutes.

Then she turned round as if she had been unaware of the Marquis, but was now looking to see if he was still there.

When she saw that he was still in the chair on the other side of the Saloon, she smiled and remarked,

"I just felt for a moment I had to get that out of me. I do hope you were not too bored, my Lord."

"Now who on earth could have taught you to play the piano like that?" the Marquis demanded.

"My mother at first, then when I was at my school I insisted on going to the leading musical professor in Paris. I am afraid it was very expensive, but he encouraged me to play what I wanted rather than the conventional pieces that the other girls were taught."

"Was that one of his compositions?"

"I wanted to say in music all I was thinking about our discussion over dinner. You know, as I do, that there are not really any words for half the issues we were trying to express."

The Marquis knew this to be true.

Yet he had never imagined he would hear them in music, which could move him as he had never been moved by music before.

"Do go on playing," he muttered.

Delia shook her head.

"No, I have said all I wanted to say and I think too I have told you all that I needed to tell you. It would be a mistake to add to it, my Lord."

The Marquis drew in his breath.

"You are undoubtedly the most extraordinary girl I have ever come across. As I have said so often before, I do not believe you are real."

"I too feel unreal, because I am wearing this lovely dress you gave me and you have told me that we are going to Greece. It is all so thrilling for me that only music can express what I have no words to say."

The Marquis rose to his feet and then their eyes met and only with the greatest difficulty did he force himself to break the spell by suggesting,

"Come outside, Delia, and let us look at the stars. Then we must retire to bed."

They walked out on deck.

It was a warm night without a breath of wind.

The moon was rising slowly up into the sky and it turned the whole of the Mediterranean to silver.

They walked in silence to the bow of the yacht and stood looking out to sea.

As well as the moon all the stars were reflected in the water.

It was all so amazingly beautiful that the Marquis and Delia just stood transfixed without speaking.

Afterwards the Marquis had no idea how long they stood there.

Then unexpectedly Delia turned and walked back to the door leading onto the deck.

Before he could speak to ask where she was going, she had vanished.

He thought for a moment that she had disappeared into the sky itself and was now one of those brilliant stars.

Then the Marquis understood, as he would not have understood before he had met Delia.

The beauty they had just seen and the music he had just heard had expressed it all.

She had known instinctively that words would only spoil total perfection.

It was all, he contemplated, so incredibly strange and something that had never happened to him before.

Yet he understood how it had all happened and in a way he had been feeling all that Delia had been feeling.

He told himself again, as he went to his cabin that she could not be real.

But she was quite right.

The only way for her to express who she really was, was in music.

# CHAPTER FIVE

The next day at breakfast the Captain was given his orders to alter course and make as fast as possible for the West coast of Greece and the Gulf of Corinth.

Delia had been out of bed early and was watching the waves breaking over the bow.

She would have loved to visit Naples.

But at present Greece was the most compelling and she was sure it would fulfil her expectations in every way.

Over breakfast the Marquis, to tease her, suggested,

"I think really you should have a look at Pompeii. After all it is one of the great sights of the world."

She did not answer but looked at him with pleading eyes.

"All right! All right! I am only teasing. We are heading straight for Greece and we'll spend as long as we dare gazing at the Goddesses who I find it hard to believe were ever as beautiful as you!"

As if he had made a joke, Delia laughed.

"Now you are flattering me, my Lord. It is only because you think I am going to be difficult about leaving Greece once we have arrived there."

"You forget I am on a mission, Delia."

"I am not likely to forget, and I am really longing to interpret Arabic for you as soon as we meet the first person speaking the language."

They went out on deck after breakfast.

"I am sure that English ship is signalling to us!" the Marquis suddenly exclaimed.

Without saying more he ran towards the bridge and because she was intrigued Delia followed him.

There was a British Destroyer apparently signalling in their direction.

"It is for us, my Lord," the Captain called out, after peering through his telescope.

"I thought it was, Captain, and I wonder why?"

It flashed through his mind that perhaps something had happened back at home that would oblige him to return immediately.

His grandmother was getting very old and he knew that he would be informed if she was dead or dying.

He could not think of any other explanation, unless the Prime Minister had changed his mind and did not want him to proceed to the Suez Canal after all.

He was still thinking of reasons why they should be intercepted when the Destroyer drew alongside the yacht.

It took a good amount of manoeuvring, but finally a large envelope was handed across to one of the crew.

The Officer on-board the Destroyer then saluted the Marquis, who took the envelope and saw it was addressed to him.

"Have you to wait for an answer?" he shouted.

The Officer shook his head.

"I've no orders to wait, my Lord."

"Thank you. It is kind of you to bring this to me."

He knew that the Captain must be curious about the contents of the letter, but he did not ask any questions.

He returned to the Saloon followed by Delia.

"What can it be?" she asked a little nervously.

The Marquis realised that she was afraid her father had found out where she was and had in some devious way persuaded the Admiralty to track her down.

Then Delia told herself that there was no need to be apprehensive.

After all, even if her father suspected the Marquis of taking her away from her home, there was no reason for him to think she was accompanying him on his yacht.

She did not say anything, but her eyes were on the Marquis as he slit open the envelope which was sealed and took out two sheets of writing paper.

On the first was written,

"*To the Marquis of Harlington.*

*My Lord,*

*The Prime Minister has sent this through to you on the private cable with instructions that we were to take it to you immediately.*"

It was signed with the name of the British Consul in Malta.

Without speaking the Marquis handed that sheet to Delia, whilst he read the other one,

"*The Khedive Ismail of Egypt has now invited their Royal Highnesses the Prince and Princess of Wales to the Opening of the Suez Canal, which he has arranged to take place on March 6th 1869.*

*Please discover who else has been invited and if, contrary to reports, the Suez Canal will be ready by then.*

*Let me have your answer as soon as possible.*

*Benjamin Disraeli.*"

The Marquis, as he read through these instructions, knew that the Prime Minister was surprised and perhaps annoyed that he had not heard from him already.

In order to please Delia, they had not hurried along on their voyage and had spent what he now realised was precious time in Gibraltar and Malta.

So it was now a question of full steam ahead.

He handed Delia the second sheet of writing paper and then he walked out of the Saloon and up to the bridge to give the Captain his new orders.

When he came back, he knew by the expression on Delia's face how disappointed she was that they would not be able to divert their course to Greece.

"We will do it on our way back," he said before she could speak.

"You promise, my Lord?"

"Of course, I promise, and I never break my word, but now we must go to work, which is what we have come for and the first thing we must do is to inspect this Canal. Personally I will be surprised if it can be finished on time, as when I last heard about it, there was little but chaos."

"It may well be true," agreed Delia. "But all those labourers working on the Suez Canal are rumoured to be performing miracles."

"Well, I rather doubt it, but we will be able to see for ourselves when we get there."

*

Two days later they arrived in the dark at the Port of Alexandria.

Delia was up early the next morning, because she was excited to see the beautiful City that had been founded by Alexander the Great.

She had read that Alexander was only twenty-five years old when in 331 BC he conquered Egypt and ordered the new Capital to be built on the Mediterranean coast.

She was looking out at the harbour they had moved into during the night, when the Marquis joined her.

"I already know without you telling me that you are thinking about Alexander the Great and that you expect me to be as powerful and as brave as he was!"

Delia laughed.

"I am not thinking about anything of the sort, but I do recall that the High Priest of the Temple of Amun hailed him as a God. I am certainly not hailing you as a God – at least not yet!"

The Marquis chuckled.

"I remember the story and when he died in Babylon of malaria, his body was brought back here to Egypt to be buried."

"But you have forgotten that then the High Priest at Memphis sent it back to Alexandria, claiming 'wherever this body may lie, the City will be uneasy, disturbed with wars and battles'."

"I can see that you are very well read, Delia, and I expect that you were also taught that in the end Alexander was buried in Soma in a tomb beneath his Temple at the main crossroads of that ancient City."

"My teacher said his body has never been found in spite of the claims of a Russian dragoman in 1850."

"I remember that too, although I was only nine at the time, but my Tutor was most interested in Alexander and told me all about the dragoman's claim. But apart from Alexander there is so much history in this City."

Delia looked at the Marquis enquiringly.

"St. Mark came here in AD 45," he then continued, "converted a Jewish shoemaker and founded the Christian Church in Alexandria. Then he was martyred for refusing to accept the Greek God of Alexandria called Serapis."

He paused and realised that Delia was listening for more and went on,

"I don't know if you were taught at School that St. Mark was buried in Alexandria, but, unlike Alexander, his remains were found hundreds of years later and smuggled out of the City, then under Arab control, in a crate of pork meat."

"I have never heard that story, my Lord!"

"It was to avoid inspection by the Moslems and he was brought to Venice, where he now rests in the famous Church of San Marco."

"That is an exciting story, but something we cannot see. Now how are we going to reach the Suez Canal?"

"The Captain has made enquiries and tells me that the nearest point to the Canal is just over one hundred and sixty miles away. I have agreed that our best plan is to sail immediately from here to Port Said, where I can inspect at least the Northern part of the Canal and its outlet into the Mediterranean."

Delia nodded her head to show that she understood, but said nothing.

"We should arrive late this evening and can spend the whole of the next day there. I would hope you will not be disappointed, but in fact, I do not think there is anything else for us to see here in Alexandria itself and certainly not as much as the Arab General who wrote in AD 642, '*I have taken the City of which I can only say that it contains 4,000 Palaces, 400 baths, 400 theatres, 1,200 greengrocers and 40,000 Jews*'!"

Delia laughed.

"How can you remember all that? Have you been swotting up on the way here, my Lord?"

"I admit I have been reading about Egypt while you

have been asleep, but actually I was made to learn that fact as a punishment at Eton when I was not attending during a history lesson!"

"It will not be so useful to us now, my Lord. Have you remembered anything more about Alexandria?"

"I can report that Napoleon Bonaparte besieged it seventy years ago, and the City surrendered to him because they knew that Cairo, which was then the centre of Egypt's wealth, learning and power, would fight on."

"I can quite see that my education will be improved by coming here with you," smiled Delia.

"And now eat your breakfast, Delia, then if you are really interested I will tell you about Florence Nightingale who was here nineteen years ago and she said scathingly – *'There is nothing in Alexandria but the Frank Square and the huts of the Alexandrians'*."

Delia laughed and they walked into breakfast.

\*

They were at sea again the whole of that day and reached Port Said late in the evening.

The next morning they hired a carriage and Delia could see the Suez Canal that there had been so much fuss about.

To her delight it was exactly as she had expected –not very broad and the land on either side was sand and not at all prepossessing.

There were a great number of men at work.

'The Babel of Nations' certainly produced a babble of voices all speaking different languages.

The Marquis knew that de Lesseps had provided for their different religions and their medical needs.

In fact, although he did not want to bore Delia with it, he had learnt that the death rate during the four years of construction was only one and a half percent a year out of over twenty thousand labourers.

The Marquis noticed was that there were two large pavilions being constructed outside Port Said.

He supposed this was where the guests who were to be expected next March would be entertained and it would certainly be in a grand and ostentatious style.

Even as he was thinking of it, an Egyptian Officer in charge of the labourers came to the side of their carriage.

"Can I be of any assistance, sir?" he asked. "I can see you are interested in the Canal."

He spoke in Arabic and the Marquis then looked at Delia.

She translated the Officer's question and told him in no uncertain terms how distinguished the Marquis was.

He then enquired if there was anything that such an important visitor would like to know about the Canal.

Delia conveyed this to the Marquis who then said he understood that the Khedive intended to open the Suez Canal next year.

Were the extremely grand pavilions being erected for the distinguished guests who would be present?

Delia translated this to the Officer.

The Marquis thought that she sounded fluent and confident in doing so.

The Officer then pointed out the places where the bands would play, the many guns fire salutes and where the Khedive would receive his guests on his yacht *Mahroussa*.

"There will be three long days of celebrations," the Officer related. "We are expecting all the Arab leaders and at least fifty men-of-war from all nations will be anchored outside the harbour."

It all sounded intriguing and Delia wished that she could be present.

While the Officer was speaking, the Marquis was looking as closely as he could at the Canal.

He was certain that it would not be too difficult in the months in between to have everything ready, at least in this section of the Canal, as the Khedive had planned.

He was also sure that if the Prince and Princess of Wales did attend as the honoured guests of the Khedive, they would be treated in great style.

He could certainly not report that the project was not significant enough for them to grace its Opening.

The Suez Canal was, in fact, he thought to himself, a miracle wrought by man.

After so much opposition and so much contention that the whole project was completely impossible, the Suez Canal was definitely viable and commercially significant.

When they had finished talking to the Officer, they drove back to Port Said.

Then Delia asked the Marquis,

"What are we going to do now?"

"We are leaving," he replied, "to sail up the nearest arm of the Nile Delta to Cairo."

"Then we can visit the Pyramids," Delia exclaimed excitedly, "and I do want to see them more than anything else."

"Of course you do, Delia, although I have seen the Pyramids once, I am perfectly prepared to see them again. But we have first to enquire if the Khedive is in residence."

"Do you mean we are going to call on him?" Delia asked, her eyes widening.

"Yes, and as you realise, I have a report to make to the Prime Minister. I think it is important for me to see the

Khedive so that I can tell the Prime Minister exactly what he wants to know."

"I am sure that you are right and am I to come with you?"

"Of course you are, after all you are my interpreter, and I am not certain whether Ismail can speak English or only French."

"I should imagine, as the English have been very unkind to him until now, he is not particularly keen on our language."

The Marquis recognised that she was right.

But he also knew, having come all this long way at the Prime Minister's request, it would be a mistake to leave before he had seen the Khedive of Egypt and if possible discovered what his intentions were once he had officially opened the Suez Canal to the world.

When they returned to *The Scimitar*, the Marquis told the Captain they wished to sail up to Cairo.

He was delighted.

"I was half afraid, my Lord, that you would wish to return home as soon as you had seen the Canal. I do not mind telling you that Cairo is a place I have always wanted to see myself, but have never had the opportunity."

"Well, I hope it does not disappoint you, Captain. Certainly there is more to see there than in Alexandria. We will take the Nile trip slowly as there is no need to hurry and I know my niece will want to admire the scenery."

"We will go slowly, my Lord, and when it is dark, we will anchor wherever we are and not push on."

The Marquis agreed to his plan.

Then he went to find Delia.

She was, as he expected, running from side to side

of the yacht to make sure she did not miss anything as they came out of port.

"I am thinking," she said, "of the enormous number of ships that will be here at the opening of the Suez Canal. You can imagine how magnificent they will look with their flags flying."

"Are you suggesting we should come back again so soon? Having seen the Suez Canal, I can think of more exciting places in the world to visit."

"And will you take me with you, even if I do not speak the language of whichever country you are visiting?"

The Marquis hesitated.

He knew it would be difficult for him to continue taking Delia with him once they had returned to England, even though she still pretended to be only fifteen.

"All right, my Lord, I know what you are thinking and I agree, it would be difficult. But it would be far more difficult for me, because when we go back, I will still not be able to return to my home."

"I realise that and I promise to find you somewhere to live, Delia, but I refuse to talk about it now."

"You are quite right, my Lord, as it would spoil this enchanting voyage which becomes more and more exciting every moment. So let us talk about Cairo and please tell me before we arrive something about it that I do not know already."

"I have an idea you know a great deal more than you pretend to, but you will certainly have the Pyramids to talk about, even if there is not as much else as you imagine there to be."

"Oh, please, it may bore you, but I want you to tell me everything you know about Cairo, just in case we miss something exciting and I will not be lucky enough to come here again."

The Marquis reckoned that was the way everyone should feel when they were about to visit a new place and he had fortunately read a great deal about Cairo apart from having visited once before.

"I would expect, Delia, you will be most interested to know that near the site of Cairo built much later by the Arabs was the ancient City of On, called by the Greeks Heliopolis, the City of the Sun. It was where the God Ra-Harakhte was worshipped, but all that is left of it is a single standing obelisk."

"Can we visit it, please?" asked Delia.

"I suppose so, but I have not seen it myself. There is also a sycamore tree, known as the 'Virgin's Tree'."

"Why is it called that?"

"Legend insists that the Virgin Mary and her Son rested beneath it during their flight from Herod. Of course, if we are honest, the tree is really a replacement for the old one that fell down in 1670, but the tree is still worshipped as the place where the Holy Family rested."

"I like that story and if it is true, then any prayers we say to it will be very special. If God is kind, we will be granted all we ask for."

"And what do you want, Delia?"

She looked away from him.

He surprised himself by feeling sure, although she was silent, that he knew the answer –

Like all women she was seeking *love*.

The love he had told himself he would never find.

It was certainly different from what was called love by the *Beau Monde* in Mayfair, and the love he himself had expressed lightly and cynically to the many women who offered him their favours.

It suddenly occurred to him that the love Delia was seeking was something especially wonderful and, perhaps one might almost say, sacred.

Then he told himself this conversation, or rather his interpretation of it, was a mistake.

"We must concentrate on the Egyptians whilst we are in Cairo," he remarked lightly. "We will have time to learn the history of the brilliant builders of the Pyramids."

"I am so excited just by the thought of seeing the Pyramids, my Lord."

Then Delia added almost as an afterthought,

"This morning when I woke up I heard the Muslims being called to prayer from the nearest Minaret. I thought how sensible it is that they should remind their people to pray before they start the day's work."

"Are you then suggesting," he enquired, "that we should build Minarets in England to alert us Christians?"

"It is certainly an idea and I thought the Muezzin's call from his Minaret – '*Allah Akbar, Allah Akbar, Allah Akbar*,' was in fact very musical."

"Then what do you suggest that Christian Priests should call out?"

"We should try to think of something appropriate and compelling, but I am afraid they would not call it and morning prayers, if they are said at all, will not be heard."

Then as they were sailing past an interesting part of the Delta, she could think of nothing but that the legendary land of Egypt was on either side of them.

She was actually here in a country she had thought she would never have the chance to visit.

They stayed the night not far from Cairo.

*

As soon as it was light, the Marquis wrote a letter to the British Consul in Cairo, Mr. Edward Rogers.

He told him he had arrived on a private visit in his yacht and that he wished to meet with the Khedive on the instructions of the Prime Minister.

He would therefore be grateful if the Consul would arrange for him to have this meeting as soon as possible.

He signed his name and sent one of the sailors, who was more intelligent than the rest, to deliver it.

The Marquis and Delia set off in an open carriage.

As the sunshine was very strong Delia was carrying a sunshade to protect her face.

As they drove into the narrow streets, the Marquis knew that she was thrilled to see the people dressed in their colourful clothes.

It took them some time to manoeuvre through the crowded streets and then to Giza where five miles further on the Great Pyramid had stood over four thousand years.

"How old is Great Pyramid?" Delia asked him.

"It was built about 2,500 BC. It was the amazing burial place built for Pharaoh Cheops, covering an area of over thirteen acres. Inside the Pyramid is Cheops's burial chamber and around the perimeter are the burial chambers of his children, courtiers and officials.

"All those around him? Why?"

"So that they might attend to him in the after-world. The ancient Egyptians, like many other races, seem to have attended no less to their Rulers after death than when they were alive."

When they arrived at the Great Pyramid, it seemed unbelievably enormous and overwhelming.

As the Marquis told her, it had been calculated that the area of its base could contain the Houses of Parliament as well as St. Paul's Cathedral and still leave a great deal of space unoccupied.

"It is fantastic," cried Delia. "I cannot imagine how they could have built all this with so few tools and none of the machines we have today that make building so much easier."

"It was said to have taken twenty years and it is still standing, while not many of our buildings have lasted more than a few hundred years!"

"It is wonderful, just wonderful and please can we go inside it."

The Marquis shook his head.

"Not now, Delia, but we will come another day and visit the other two Pyramids, one of which is almost as big as the Great Pyramid and the Sphinx as well.

"We must return now just in case there is a message about meeting the Khedive. It would be extremely rude, if, after having asked to meet him, we were either late or so careless as to miss the appointment altogether."

"Yes, I do understand, my Lord."

If there was one thing he really liked about this girl, he reflected, it was that she was always reasonable about anything suggested to her.

The women he had known in the past were usually most unreasonable – so that he had found himself on many occasions on the verge of losing his temper.

When they reached the yacht, Delia claimed that he must have been using his *Third Eye* because they found the invitation waiting for them.

It was that the Khedive Ismail would be delighted to receive the Marquis at five o'clock that afternoon.

The Marquis felt that he had almost won a battle, as he was quite certain that if he had gone to the Consulate himself, it would have taken longer and he would have had to explain to the Consul the full reasons for his request.

At once Delia asked him breathlessly,

"Am I coming with you, my Lord?"

"Of course you are, Delia, so put on your prettiest dress. As you are English, they will expect you to wear a hat, but if you were an Arab, you would have to cover not only your head but also your face."

"I am so thankful I am not one!" exclaimed Delia. "It must be terribly hot wearing one of those yashmaks in this heat. Also, if you are pretty, it is very sad that no one can see your face!"

"Except your husband. And as the Khedive has a goodly number of wives, he would judge your appearance critically."

Delia laughed.

She changed her dress into one she considered the prettiest of all they had bought and wore a hat that matched the gown.

They arrived at the Palace in Cairo where a crowd of servants were ready to greet them.

They were escorted with much pomp through many rooms until finally the Marquis and Delia were taken into a room where the Khedive was waiting.

It was not a surprise to the Marquis, although it was to Delia, that the room looked exactly like any study they would find in an English ancestral house.

The Marquis knew that the Khedive was an admirer of all things European.

He was small and ugly but, as the Marquis had been told, had an unmistakable charm and like most Egyptians, he looked older than he actually was.

He greeted the Marquis most effusively.

And only after the Marquis had spoken to him in a complimentary manner of the progress he had made with the Suez Canal, did he say,

"I hope, Your Highness, I may introduce my niece who is accompanying me. She is as impressed as I am by the marvellous speed in which you have accomplished so much in so little time."

The Khedive accepted the introduction, but he was obviously not interested in a young woman.

Instead he indicated two large chairs close to each other where he and the Marquis could sit and talk.

They were at the moment speaking French and the Marquis had learnt that the Khedive was quite fluent in the language.

Now as they sat down, he commented,

"I am very sorry but I cannot speak Arabic, Your Highness, although my niece strangely enough learnt it at school from an Egyptian girl. She will interpret anything you wish to say to me in your own language."

The Khedive looked surprised.

Then, as if he was testing the Marquis, he spoke to Delia.

He asked her in Arabic if this was her first visit to Egypt.

She then answered him in the flowery language the Egyptians were so proud of, saying that she was overcome, astonished and rendered speechless at the miracle he had accomplished in building the Suez Canal.

She went on to tell him how thrilled she was by the magnificence of the Great Pyramid.

The Khedive was delighted and clapped his hands as Delia finished speaking.

"She is very good," he said to the Marquis and then he realised he was speaking in Arabic and hastily translated it into French.

The Marquis asked him, without making it sound as if he was prying, what was his ambition for the future.

The Khedive then burst into an animated reply that revealed how obsessed he was – to the point that he could scarcely express his feelings. He stumbled over his words and used his hands even more than usual to illustrate all he was trying to say.

Talking in a strange mixture of French and Arabic, he explained just how he intended to transform Cairo into a European City.

He believed that only the Europeans could help him achieve this and that he would eventually make Egypt itself into a European country.

The Marquis was astonished at this revelation and he was clever enough to spur the Khedive on.

He learnt that the Khedive's chief ambition was to achieve more independence from Turkey and to implement his grandfather's plan to conquer the whole of the Sudan and its outlying areas.

"In other words," he intoned solemnly almost as if he was making an oath, "I want Egypt to be at the head of an African Empire."

It was a notion, the Marquis mused, that the Prime Minister knew nothing about.

He then asked the Khedive if he thought his people would be content with such a change.

"My country and my people," he replied, "are no longer in Africa, they are in Europe!"

He spoke so positively that it was impossible, the Marquis decided, to argue the point.

He then became aware that the Khedive was hinting that he needed British assistance for Egypt to seek financial independence from the French.

After all that had been said and done in the past the Marquis found this astounding, but he was clever enough not to let Ismail realise how much it surprised him.

He was also aware that Delia was listening intently to every word and he felt sure that when overcome with his own excitement, the Khedive would break into Arabic and she could memorise and tell him later exactly what he had said.

It seemed to him astonishing that after many years of hostility to the British, the Egyptians should now want to change direction so completely –

To become as the Khedive insisted – Europeans rather than Africans.

'Is it possible,' he wondered, 'that the Egyptians could become content with such a fundamental change?'

All the Marquis could do at this early stage was to promise the Khedive that he would speak with the Prime Minister about his ambitions.

He felt sure that Mr. Disraeli would be more than interested.

"I think that you should know, Your Highness, that Mr. Disraeli is now extremely sorry that he did not support the building of the Suez Canal when it was first proposed by de Lesseps. I am sure now he will be only too willing to help you to achieve all you desire for Egypt."

He saw the Khedive's eyes light up and carried on,

"I will tell him exactly all you have said. There is one matter which the Prime Minister especially now feels sad about. That is that Britain has no financial interest in the Suez Canal."

The Khedive was quick-witted and the Marquis did not need to say any more.

Now speaking in Arabic the Khedive answered,

"That may come somewhat later, but like all good things it will come."

"I understand, Your Highness, and I can only thank you again for granting me this audience. I promise I will do everything in my power to assist you in achieving your great ambition."

The Khedive was delighted.

He rose to his feet and clapped his hands, bringing servants running into the room.

He ordered coffee to be brought and then spoke to one of the senior servants in a quiet tone of voice.

Delia realised he was asking for presents to give to them and she managed to whisper this to the Marquis.

He nodded to say that he understood and when the presents appeared, he was suitably surprised.

He then thanked the Khedive a thousand times for his unbounded generosity.

They sat sipping the thick sweet coffee.

Because she was a woman, the Khedive did not say anything to Delia except to tell her to explain something to the Marquis that he could only express in Arabic.

When they rose to leave, the Marquis thanked him once again for his kindness and for the presents.

Delia curtsied as she had done when they arrived.

He patted her gently on the shoulder and said that she was a good little girl.

She accepted this as a compliment, aware that if she had been Egyptian, she would have kissed his feet.

They were escorted by the servants to the front door of the Palace and their carriage was waiting outside.

As the servants bowed and they drove away, Delia exclaimed,

"I just cannot believe that really happened. He is the most extraordinary man I have ever seen. Now I must tell you, my Lord, what he said in Arabic when he was so excited."

"I kept feeling so thankful that you were with me, Delia, and now you can tell me word for word all that he said. You realise how important it is."

# CHAPTER SIX

By the evening she had told the Marquis everything the Khedive had said in Arabic and then Delia admitted to being quite weary and they had an early night.

The next morning, as soon as she had greeted the Marquis at breakfast, Delia asked him eagerly,

"Now, what are we going to do today, my Lord?"

"I know perfectly well you want to go sightseeing, and I suppose I will have to climb the Great Pyramid!"

"You did promise me we could go inside."

"Very well, Delia, but you will find it very airless and uncomfortable, especially as one has to crawl part of the way. At the same time when you go back to England you can boast you have done it."

Delia nearly enquired, 'who to?' and then she felt it would be drawing too much attention to her own troubles.

Instead she admitted,

"You are so kind, my Lord, and I am sorry to be a bore, but I do want to see some of Cairo whilst I am here."

"Well, you should see Shepheard's Hotel – "

Delia looked surprised and then she asked,

"Why is it particularly interesting?"

"It is the most famous hotel in the Middle East. It was founded by Samuel Shepheard and it is patronised by the most important British visitors besides all the Officers of any Regiment in the vicinity."

He just prevented himself from adding ' – and all the prettiest girls.'

Delia was puzzled as to why a hotel should be of so much interest.

There were many Ancient Egyptian buildings she had not yet seen especially the Sphinx.

She was to learn later that people who patronised Shepheard's used to sit at tables outside and claimed they saw 'the world pass by'!

What the Marquis did not tell her was that Samuel Shepheard had actually sold the hotel in 1861 for about ten thousand pounds and had returned home to England.

Yet he had done considerably more than just secure a comfortable old age for himself and his family – as for many travellers his name had become a symbol of style and service that never disappeared from Shepheard's.

The Marquis thought perhaps they might go there for dinner and then he remembered that any English people there might know who he was.

They would undoubtedly think it rather strange that he was with a beautiful young girl with long golden hair.

Once again Delia was reading his thoughts.

"You must go there alone if you want to, my Lord. I think it might be dangerous for me to accompany you."

"You are so right, Delia. When you have finished breakfast I will take you on a drive round Cairo. There are some very fine Mosques that will interest you."

He smiled at her as he carried on,

"After luncheon we will go back to Giza for you to see the Great Pyramid once again. If you are not too long crawling around inside it, we might go and see the Sphinx and the two other Pyramids beside it."

"I would love to," she exclaimed, "and perhaps you and I will guess what the Sphinx is really thinking. No one has been able to answer that question yet."

The Marquis smiled at her, he liked her enthusiasm.

He thought how few women he had known in the past would have been far more excited at crawling inside a Pyramid than being alone with him!

After their drive around Cairo, which Delia found entrancing, they returned to a delicious luncheon.

They had just finished when the Steward came into the Saloon and handed the Marquis a card.

"This has just arrived, my Lord, and the man who brought it indicates that he's waiting for an answer."

The Marquis took the card.

On it was written in large letters,

"*His Excellency Vizier Ahmed.*"

The Marquis stared at it and asked Delia,

"I wonder who this is. Please read what is written underneath."

Delia then translated the words in Arabic under the name of Vizier Ahmed.

"It says will you call on him immediately as it is of the greatest importance."

"I wonder what he can mean by that?"

"Vizier is next to the Khedive in rank," said Delia. "He is higher than a Pasha."

The Marquis realised that it must be someone really distinguished.

"I suppose I shall have to go if he wants to see me, and as he obviously speaks only Arabic, you must come as well."

"Of course I will come with you, my Lord, after all, I am your interpreter."

"I doubt if anyone looking at you would believe it," the Marquis chuckled as she ran to her cabin to change.

Ten minutes later he thought she was particularly attractive with her hair curling over her pretty white dress.

It was the expensive one she had kept for important occasions like visiting the Khedive.

And now she decided that the same dress would be appropriate too for the next in line.

"I do hope it will not take long, my Lord. I suppose you will want to send a message to the Prime Minister."

"I am not certain whether I would be comfortable in sending any confidential message from Cairo. I may have to wait till we reach a more civilised country like Greece."

Delia smiled.

"So you have not forgotten you promised we would call in there on our return journey."

"Of course not, Delia. As I have told you before, I always keep my promises."

"I think that is one of the nicest things about you, my Lord. You only say things that you believe and if you say you will do something you will never go back on your word."

"Thank you indeed, Delia. I am very grateful for this appreciation of my character!"

Delia laughed.

"I know that you think I am presumptuous and that I should keep my place as a mere woman, but I find myself expressing myself just as the thoughts come into my mind. You did tell me, when we first talked about it, it was what you wanted me to do."

"Of course, I want you to do so and I still find it so extraordinary, Delia, that you think so much and are so perceptive."

"How could we be anything else in Egypt? We all have something to learn from the Egyptians although we do not admit it."

"If nothing else – how to build a Pyramid!"

Delia smiled.

"I hope we will not need to do so. But perhaps the Sphinx will be able to tell me the answer to my problems, my Lord."

The Marquis knew that she was still worried about what would happen to her when they returned to England, but he thought it a mistake to discuss it now and he merely replied,

"I will send a message to the Vizier, whoever he may be, to say we will call on him in half-an-hour's time."

He told the Steward to convey this to the man who had brought the Vizier's card.

They were drinking their coffee when the Steward came back to say,

"There's a carriage outside, my Lord, and the man driving it says he expects you to travel with him back to his Master."

The Marquis frowned.

"That would be a great mistake."

"Yes, indeed it would," Delia agreed quickly. "We would not be able to leave when we wished even though he would undoubtedly bring us straight back to the yacht."

The Marquis smiled.

"And avoiding naturally, the Sphinx and the Great Pyramid!"

"Oh, please," she pleaded, "let's say we will follow his carriage to where the Vizier lives."

"That is just what I am going to do," the Marquis answered. "You have taken the words out of my mouth."

He was on the point of instructing the Steward to take this message when he intervened,

"Excuse me, my Lord, but I do thinks it'll be very difficult to make the man driving the carriage understand. He told me what to convey to you by waving his hands and pointing."

"I will go and tell him," suggested Delia.

She rose from the table.

Almost before the Marquis was aware of what she was about to do, she was out on deck and running down the gangway.

He followed her slowly, thinking that whatever else might happen she was still determined to continue with her sightseeing.

At the same time he really enjoyed and appreciated her enthusiasm.

She was so completely unlike all the other women who had travelled with him.

They only wanted to go on shore to visit the shops and they usually found even the most famous sights a bore.

Standing on deck he could see the carriage that had been sent for him – it was an open chaise, well built and drawn by two well-bred horses.

It was obvious that the Vizier could afford the best.

He also saw there was one man driving and another talking to Delia, both of them in some sort of livery.

He had to admit that the carriage they had hired to visit the Khedive the previous afternoon was very shabby in comparison.

Equally he instinctively knew that Delia was right, as if they once accepted the Vizier's hospitality, they might be marooned in his Palace, or wherever he lived, for hours on end and unable to leave when they wanted.

She was smiling as she came back up the gangway to where the Marquis was waiting for her.

"I have told him that we will follow him because we have somewhere we must visit after we have seen the Vizier."

Delia sighed before she continued,

"He was upset that we would not go in his carriage, and did not trust our driver not to get lost in the crowded streets and miss the way."

"I know exactly what is worrying you," smiled the Marquis. "You are afraid that darkness will fall before you have had time to talk to the Sphinx."

"Now you are reading my thoughts again!"

"But you are quite right, Delia. Now please put on your hat, because you know women are not allowed to be uncovered in an Oriental City and I do promise I will try to cut short our conversation with this Vizier. I suspect, in fact, that you will be doing the talking more than I will!"

"Then I will be sure to cut him short, my Lord. The Orientals make incredibly long speeches, especially when they are impressed by someone like you."

"Come back and finish your coffee, Delia. Quite frankly if I have to endure another endless half and half conversation with you translating, then I insist on having a liqueur before I leave!"

"I do wish we did not have to go, but I suppose it would be rude not to. Also, as he obviously knows who you are, my Lord, he will undoubtedly know all about our visit to the Khedive yesterday afternoon."

The Marquis sat down and ordered himself a *crème de menthe*.

"I have been told it is a mistake," Delia remarked mischievously, "to drink alcohol when it is hot."

"If it was the summer heat you would be right," the Marquis replied, "but as it happens it is hardly any hotter today than it would be in England. Therefore I do intend to enjoy myself."

Delia put her elbows on the dining room table and rested her chin in her hands.

"Are you really enjoying yourself, my Lord?" she asked him. "And would you be happier if I was not with you?"

"I will answer your question entirely truthfully and you will have to believe me, Delia."

"Yes, of course – "

"Very well. I thought when I took you aboard that I should be bored stiff with having such a young girl with me. Instead of which I have quite frankly enjoyed every minute, and I have been amazed at our conversation, which I would only have expected to have with a man of my own age or even a younger one brighter and wiser than me."

Delia put down her hands.

"Thank you! Thank you! my Lord, I was so afraid that I was being a bore about seeing the sights and that you were really anxious to return home as soon as possible."

"If I wanted to, I would have told you so. Actually I am in no hurry and there are lots of other places we might travel to besides Greece."

Delia's eyes were shining.

"Do you really mean it, my Lord? You are not just saying it to make me happy."

"I am saying it because it is the truth," the Marquis replied. "I find you, Delia, and again I am being truthful, one of the most interesting people I have ever met."

She glanced at the Marquis quizzically to see if he was laughing at her and then she said in a quiet little voice,

"You have made me very happy, my Lord."

"You must not worry too much about your future, Delia, I have a distinct feeling that it will take care of itself. It is always a mistake to be in too much of a hurry in life."

His voice changed as he added,

"Let us wait and see what happens and maybe we will find a solution that is totally different from anything we can think of at this particular moment."

"What I would love to do more than anything," she whispered, "is to go on exploring the world and talking to you about it all endlessly."

Then before the Marquis could reply, she put up her hands.

"Don't say anything, I know I should not have said it. It was greedy and presumptuous of me, but it just came out before I could stop it!"

The Marquis chuckled.

"I think that we are both being too serious, which is quite unnecessary at the moment. You are safe from your father at present and I am finding you just the interpreter I wanted. Undoubtedly I shall need one this afternoon."

"I think you are wonderful," Delia sighed. "Now I am going to put on my hat and make myself look like a respectable woman."

She rose from the table and without waiting for the Marquis to open the door, she let herself out of the Saloon.

He was smiling as he finished his liqueur.

In her cabin Delia brushed her hair and tidied it and then she picked up the hat she had thrown down on the bed after she had returned this morning from their drive.

She had hoped that this afternoon she would be able to go bareheaded to the Pyramids and the Sphinx.

But she was only too well aware that any important Egyptian would think it a gross insult if her head was not covered in his presence.

Fortunately her hat that matched the dress was most attractive and when she looked at herself in the mirror she decided that she looked pretty but very young – not a day older than fifteen.

She had a sudden impulse to put up her hair and be her age.

She was, however, certain the Marquis was used to thinking that she was still a child.

She wanted him to think about her, apart from her brain, as being grown-up.

Then she told herself she was asking too much.

She had been so lucky in finding someone as kind and considerate as the Marquis.

He had saved her from being beaten until she was unconscious and married to the horrible Comte her father had chosen for her.

'I am lucky, so incredibly lucky,' she murmured to herself.

Then she asked herself why she was thinking about all this at this particular moment.

She had been feeling most unselfconscious in the last few days.

It had been a joy yesterday to be able to translate what the Khedive had said.

'The Marquis is really finding me useful,' she told herself. 'So I hope he will be in no hurry to get rid of me.'

At the same time they would have to return home to England sooner or later.

Then would come the terrifying question of where she would go and where she could hide.

'I will not think about this dreadful problem now,' she told her reflection in the mirror firmly.

Yet she knew, however hard she tried to eliminate it, that it was always there at the back of her mind.

It was like a dark cloud waiting to enfold her.

She turned away from the mirror and collected her gloves which she had also thrown on the bed.

If she was herself and not disguised as a young girl she would have taken a handbag, but as she had no money it was unnecessary.

Anyway at fifteen a girl did not require the aids to beauty that were permitted for *debutantes*.

When she went up the companionway towards the Saloon, the Marquis commented,

"You have been titivating for a long time. Come on, let us get this tiresome visit over with and then we can enjoy ourselves."

Delia smiled at him.

"I am praying it will not take too long, my Lord."

"I will add my prayers to yours as well, Delia, and they should be doubly effective!"

They walked down the gangway.

Despite low bows from the Vizier's servants, they climbed into the carriage they had ordered for themselves.

The horses moved off.

The Marquis made himself comfortable by putting his feet on the seat opposite.

"I only hope the Vizier does not live far outside the City," he remarked. "Maybe you should have asked where we are going."

"I did not think of it at the time, my Lord, and now it is too late."

"I have always thought those are particularly dismal words," the Marquis muttered. "We may have to prepare ourselves for an hour's journey – "

"Oh, I do hope not, my Lord."

They travelled for a while in silence and then Delia suddenly remarked,

"I have a feeling this interview or whatever it is, is going to be a dangerous one."

"Why do you say that, Delia?"

"I don't know, but I feel it somehow. The warning, if that is what it is, is coming to me from the carriage in front of us."

"I think you are just telling yourself a fairy tale. As you heard yesterday, the Khedive is wooing Europeans and is most anxious to befriend us. You told me he offered to arrange for us any entertainment we desired while we were in Cairo and has also invited us personally to the Opening of the Suez Canal."

"Naturally he wants you to be there, my Lord. The more aristocratic English he can attract, the more it will delight him, and I should imagine that it will also delight the Prime Minister."

"I will be very glad when the Canal is finished, but I have no wish to be a guest at the Opening. I can imagine only too well what it will be like and quite frankly I find all that kind of celebration and speech-making a bore."

"I guessed you would say that," Delia smiled.

The Marquis turned his head and saw that she was staring nervously at the carriage in front of them.

She put out her hand and laid it on his arm.

"I am frightened," she murmured. "I don't really know why, but I am."

"There is no need to be frightened, Delia, I promise you this Egyptian is not going to hurt us. Why should he? If he opposes the policy of the Khedive, I am quite certain by this time he would have been sacked or pushed aside. The Egyptians are never very kind to their enemies."

"Therefore it must be silly of me," Delia said after a moment's pause, "but I am using my *Third Eye* and I know something is very wrong."

"Very well, shall I order the men to turn and drive back?"

"No, of course not. I am just being over-sensitive. Why should I be scared of anything when I am with you?"

"Without being conceited, Delia, I did save a lot of lives when I was in India simply because I knew with what you call my *Third Eye* that something dangerous was going to happen."

Delia made a little murmur, but before she could speak the Marquis finished,

"At the moment I do not feel as I felt then, so I can assure you that your fears are quite unnecessary."

"And I am with you, my Lord, and that is really all that matters."

The Marquis did not answer her, but he thought she was being more imaginative than usual.

He could understand her in a way as the Oriental background was sometimes disconcerting to very sensitive people.

In the past there had been so much bloodshed and trouble in Cairo and the atmosphere was so very different from an ordinary English City.

They drove on and on until they passed through the City and into the Southern suburbs.

It was then, as the Marquis was beginning to worry

in case they still had a long way to go, they came to some large gates.

They were the entrance to a most imposing house.

"We have arrived," he said to Delia, "and I am very grateful to find that we have not any further to go."

"I am grateful too," she agreed, "and if this is his Palace, it is certainly a very attractive one."

The gardens were a mass of flowers and the trees were in blossom and in the far distance they could see the Pyramids.

The gates were opened by two men wearing a kind of uniform.

As they drove up to the front door of the house, the Marquis noticed that it was even larger than he had thought when he first saw it.

Judging by the mob of servants who hurried down the steps as the carriages ground to a standstill, no expense was clearly spared in keeping up appearances.

Delia climbed out first and then stood back to allow the Marquis to precede her.

A senior servant, obviously a major-domo arrayed in even more impressive livery, bowed politely.

In broken French he asked them to follow him.

He led them through a number of different rooms, each one more elaborately furnished in the Oriental style than the last.

There was no touch of European style here, as there had been in the Khedive's Palace.

Finally they came to a room where there were no sofas or armchairs – only stools with a cushion that were always provided for those who ate in an Oriental house.

There was fruit and large bowls of sweetmeats on the tables.

The major-domo then invited them to sit down and be served.

The Marquis glanced at Delia and she said to him in Arabic,

"It is most gracious of His Excellency to offer us food. But you will understand we only finished luncheon recently and are therefore not hungry."

Even as she spoke servants came hurrying into the room with coffee, poured it out and set the cups in front of them.

"His Excellency invites you to eat and drink with him as a gesture of his friendship before he receives you," the major-domo intoned in Arabic.

Then bowing almost to the ground he moved out of the room.

"This is most unusual," the Marquis hissed in a low voice.

"I think it would be a mistake to drink the coffee, in fact I know it would be," Delia whispered back.

The Marquis looked at her in surprise.

"Are you suggesting it is drugged?"

"I don't know. I only have this distinct feeling that something is very wrong and I know that we should *not* be here."

"Very well, Delia, I naturally respect your instinct and anyway I dislike Egyptian coffee. It is too heavy and too sweet."

"I wonder how long they will give us to drink it."

"Maybe we will have to wait until we have finished it," the Marquis suggested teasingly.

"I would pour it on the floor, my Lord, if I did not think we were being watched!"

"I am certain you are right there, Delia, it would be best not to make a mess."

"I will tell you what we should do, my Lord, stir the coffee and then put a spoonful or two into the saucer. They will think you have drunk some of it at any rate."

The Marquis considered that she was being almost hysterical, but he had no wish to argue with her.

He therefore did as she suggested. And she did too.

It certainly reduced the amount in the cups, but it was, however, obvious to anyone looking closely that there was a great deal of coffee in the saucers.

"I just don't know why," Delia muttered nervously, "but I feel as if the walls are closing in on us."

"I don't know what has come over you, Delia. You were perfectly happy yesterday and you did not have this strange feeling when we went to visit the Khedive."

"Yes, I know. But all the way here I felt something was wrong and something very unpleasant lay ahead. Now we are here the feeling is even more intense than it was before."

"What I ought to have said to you a long time ago, Delia, is that you must not let these psychic feelings get too strong a hold of you. I have often thought in the past that people who indulge in fortune-telling and the occult often become weird themselves, simply because they are playing about with the unknown."

"I understand what you are saying to me, my Lord, but I cannot control my feelings."

She gave a deep sigh and then continued,

"Just as I knew when I was running away from my Papa and climbed into the box at the back of your chaise that you would help me – and that it was the right thing to do, even though Papa would be furious with me."

"I am sure, but at the same time, as I have already said, it is a mistake to let anything get hold of you. I have met a few people on my travels who have been psychic or who have dedicated themselves to becoming Holy men.

"For them, life is completely different from ours. In fact they seem to exist on another planet and, to put it simply, are rather mad!"

"I promise you I won't go mad," Delia exclaimed. "If I was wise, maybe I would not talk of my feelings. But in my view it is only right that you should hear them and be prepared for something strange and perhaps unpleasant to happen."

"Now I think you are just frightening yourself," the Marquis replied. "I might listen to you if we were in India, but as you heard yesterday the Khedive is so determined to make this City as European as Paris or London. But I can assure you that the women here are nothing like so pretty or approachable!"

He had meant Delia to laugh and she did.

"No, of course it is not a bit like Paris or London and never will be. There is an Oriental atmosphere here that is inescapable and however hard the Khedive tries he is not going to alter that."

"I would hope not," he agreed. "I like every City to be itself and it is ridiculous of the Khedive to think he can change the Orient or even identify Egypt with Europe."

The Marquis was speaking in a low voice and Delia looked nervously across the room just in case anyone was listening.

"The Khedive is absolutely convinced that is what he will do," she whispered, "but I think the owner of this Palace has very different ideas."

"It looks as it should look and I would suggest that we should congratulate him on it."

"I will try to make it a very short speech!"

The Marquis laughed.

As he spoke the major-domo returned.

"His Excellency the Vizier will see you now," he said in broken French bowing to the Marquis.

The Marquis rose to his feet and put out his hand towards Delia.

"Come along," he urged, "it will not be as bad as you anticipate and we have our own carriage outside."

He was speaking so quietly that it would have been difficult for the major-domo to hear, even if he understood English.

He led them along a wide passage with little light as there were no windows.

They walked for quite a long way and at the far end of the passage the major-domo paused.

He waited with his hand on a door which he did not open until the Marquis and Delia joined him.

Then he opened it wide and intoned in a loud voice in Arabic,

"Your guests are here, Your Excellency, and may they prostrate themselves before you."

Ahead of them the Marquis could see a very large room in completely Oriental style and there were a number of thick rugs on the floor.

There was a subdued light from windows that were veiled with elaborate silk curtains.

At the far end of the room seated in a chair, which could easily have been a throne, there was a man.

As they advanced towards him, they heard the door close behind them.

The Marquis was aware that the Vizier was dressed

entirely in Oriental clothes with a long silk robe falling to the ground and he was wearing a red fez on his head.

As they drew nearer, and it was quite a long walk from the door to where the Vizier was seated, he rose to his feet and waited for them to reach him.

As they did so, Delia suddenly gave a loud scream and threw out her hands towards the Marquis.

"*It is the – Comte,*" she cried incoherently.

The Marquis turned to look at her in astonishment and then as she came to a standstill, he stopped too.

As he did so the Vizier snarled,

"Yes, Delisia, it is the Comte, and I have found you again as I intended."

The Marquis grasped the situation at once.

As he looked at the Vizier he knew only too clearly why Delia had been terrified and disgusted at having this monster forced on her as her husband.

He was small, dark and swarthy.

His face certainly did not betray much of his French blood and wearing his Egyptian robes he looked absolutely and completely Oriental.

With the swiftness of brain that had served him so well in the past, the Marquis decided at once how to handle the situation they now found themselves in.

He began in French,

"It is a pleasure to meet you, Your Excellency, but it appears my interpreter knows you already."

"She does indeed," the Vizier replied now speaking in English, "because her father arranged that she should be my wife. Yet on the day I arrived at Lord Durham's house, his daughter had just disappeared, apparently in the back of your chaise that had been waiting for you outside the front door."

The Marquis stared at him as if he was completely bewildered.

"I don't understand, Your Excellency, are you now telling me that this young girl, who offered her services to me as an interpreter, is the daughter of my neighbour and friend Lord Durham."

"Are you saying, my Lord, you were not aware of that fact?"

"Of course I was not aware of it," the Marquis said sharply. "On my way to London I stopped twice at posting inns for refreshment and when I reached my yacht to sail to Egypt, this young woman appeared from the back of my chaise begging me to take her with me to wherever I was going."

The Vizier was clearly surprised at this story, but he persisted,

"But surely, my Lord, you did not agree to such an extraordinary suggestion."

"I did my best to tell her that I had no intention of taking her on my yacht, but she said she had learnt I was travelling to Egypt and offered herself as an interpreter.

"I had in fact been looking for one and had asked the Prime Minister to supply me with a man, unfortunately he had been unable to find one for me."

"So you had no idea that this was Lord Durham's daughter?" the Vizier demanded, as if he must be sure that the Marquis was telling him the truth.

"Of course I had no idea," the Marquis responded scornfully. "Do you really imagine I would insult such a close neighbour and friend as Lord Durham? But this girl was most insistent, and my inability to speak a single word of Arabic put me, as you might understand, in a somewhat uncomfortable position regarding my diplomatic mission."

The Vizier nodded and the Marquis went on,

"I then allowed her to come with me and I can only say that when I visited the Khedive yesterday morning, as you will know, she performed her duties most admirably."

"She did not tell you that she was promised to me as my wife?" the Vizier rasped.

"Not at all. If I had had any idea that she was her father's daughter, I would have refused to take her. In fact, I am deeply shocked at her deceitfulness. At the same time I must say that she speaks Arabic fluently, which has been extremely useful to me on my mission."

"Although, I speak French and English as fluently as Arabic," the Vizier added, "I like my women to talk to me when they are here in the language of my country."

The Marquis smiled.

"I can understand that, Your Excellency."

He had been watching the Vizier closely as he was talking and he was quite certain that he was concealing a weapon, probably a revolver, in his right hand.

It was very difficult for an Egyptian to talk for long without waving his hands.

As the Vizier had used his left hand to gesticulate freely, he had kept his right down at his side.

The Marquis was now wondering desperately what he could do, and how he could spirit Delia away from the Vizier's clutches.

Then as he felt her hand, which was still on his arm, tremble, he turned to her savagely,

"How did you manage to deceive me so cleverly? Why did you not tell me you were running away from your father?"

He knew as he spoke that she would be intelligent enough to play up to him.

She replied in an almost pitiful voice,

"You must please forgive me, my Lord, but I was disturbed because I had no wish to marry anyone and I had intended, if you had not taken me to Egypt to act as your interpreter, to enter a Convent and become a nun."

"I think that would have been a ridiculous thing to do," the Marquis said, "and I am sure that His Excellency would think, as I do, that you are far too pretty to be a nun.

"Anyway I am certain that His Excellency is as disgusted by your behaviour and the lies you have told me, as I am. I will therefore take you back and hand you over to your father, who will deal with you as he thinks fit – "

He saw a light flash into Delia's eyes as she looked up at him.

He knew that she thought he was being very astute.

Then the Vizier intervened,

"Wait a minute! This young woman was promised to me and although I think she has behaved badly and she must accept some sort of punishment, I am still prepared to take her as my wife."

For a moment the Marquis was silent and then he responded,

"That is most generous of Your Excellency and I can only commend you for being so very considerate. I have fortunately finished my business to Egypt and I must return to England at once. I can, of course, leave Miss Durham safely in your hands."

The Vizier, who had been looking stern, smiled for the first time.

"That is exactly what I desire, my Lord."

The Marquis felt Delia trembling, but she did not speak.

He stepped forward towards the Vizier holding out his hand.

As he had anticipated the Vizier had been holding something beneath his robes and he now dropped it into the chair behind him.

He turned round sweeping back his robes so that he could take the Marquis's hand.

The Marquis moved forward.

With the expertise of a pugilist he caught the Vizier a cracking blow on the chin that knocked him backwards.

As he stumbled, the Marquis struck him again on the chest.

He fell sideways against his chair, hitting his head against its wooden arm.

When his body reached the floor he was completely unconscious.

The Marquis took a quick look at him.

Then taking Delia by the hand he walked rapidly across the room and opened the door.

As he expected the major-domo and another servant were waiting outside.

"Tell him we brought the Vizier some bad news," he hissed to Delia, "and that he wishes to be left alone."

With, he thought, commendable self-control Delia translated this into Arabic and added,

"I would not disturb your Master now for at least an hour. He is very upset at what we have just told him."

The major-domo led them back to their carriage.

They deliberately walked slowly as if they were in no hurry and when they reached the carriage they stepped inside it quite calmly while the servants bowed.

As soon as they were outside the gates and they had closed, Delia threw herself against the Marquis.

"You – saved me!" she burst out. "How could you be – so brilliant?"

Then as she stammered the last words she burst into tears.

# CHAPTER SEVEN

The Marquis pulled off Delia's hat and put his arms around her.

For a moment he held her close against him without speaking.

Then as soon as he realised they were out of sight of the gates of the Vizier's Palace, he gently took his arms from around her.

Rising, he stood on the seat opposite to speak to the driver and ordered him to go swiftly to the British Consul's Palace.

The man repeated the address after him and nodded to say he understood.

He went back to Delia.

She was still crying and had covered her face with both hands.

He took her in his arms and said to her softly,

"It is all over and no one will hurt you. That swine will never come near you ever again."

"But – he will," Delia sobbed. "He will come back to England again – I know he will."

"By the time we reach English it will be impossible for him to touch you. That I promise you, my darling."

As he spoke he felt her stiffen.

She took her hands away from her face.

The Marquis looked down at her, thinking that even

136

with tears dappling her cheeks and trickling from her eyes, she looked indescribably lovely and ethereal.

"That devil will never upset you again," promised the Marquis quietly, "and you have to trust me."

"But how can you – stop him?"

The Marquis smiled.

"I am going to stop him in such a way that you will never be frightened by him again."

"How can that be possible?" she pleaded.

"*Because we are going to the Consul's Palace now to be married.*"

Delia's blue eyes seemed to fill her whole face as she looked up at the Marquis and repeated almost beneath her breath.

"*Married?*"

"I love you," the Marquis breathed. "Do you really think I could lose you to any man, least of all someone as despicable as him? You are mine, Delia, and I will never lose you."

"I think – I am dreaming – " Delia murmured as if she was about to faint.

But her eyes were shining and he felt that no one could look more radiant or breathtakingly beautiful.

"I love you," the Marquis continued, "and later on I will tell you how much. But the Consul's Palace is not far away. In fact we are almost there now."

He drew a handkerchief from his pocket.

He handed it to Delia and she wiped her eyes.

As she did so, they turned in at a pair of large and stately gates.

Ahead, as the Marquis remembered, was the Palace he had visited some years ago when he had been in Cairo.

He took his arms from around Delia as they passed the sentries at the gates who presented arms.

Then as they drew nearer to the large house set in an ornamental garden, Delia reached out for her hat.

As she picked it up, she looked questioningly at the Marquis.

"You did – say," she stuttered, "that you would not marry – anyone."

"I have every intention of marrying you, Delia, and when we are alone and leaving Cairo as quickly as we can, I will tell you why."

For a moment their eyes gazing into the other's said a great deal without ant need for words.

Then as the carriage stopped, the Marquis stepped out first.

As Delia followed him an Englishman appeared at the door and the Marquis ran up the steps towards him.

"I am the Marquis of Harlington and I wish to see the Consul immediately. It is vitally important."

"I am sure that he will be delighted to see you, my Lord," replied the Englishman.

The Marquis hesitated and then he added,

"The lady accompanying me has suffered rather a traumatic experience and I would be grateful if she could go somewhere to tidy herself while I speak to the Consul."

"I am sure that Mrs. Rogers would be delighted to look after her."

Then as they moved into the hall an *aide-de-camp* appeared and bowed to them.

The Englishman they had met first said,

"This lady is accompanying Lord Harlington whom I am taking to His Excellency's office. Would you be very kind and take her to Mrs. Rogers so she can tidy herself."

Delia looked in a desperate way at the Marquis as if she was afraid to leave him.

"It will not be for long, Delia, and I am sure you would like to tidy your hair."

Delia suddenly remembered that her hair was loose and that she should still be looking only fifteen.

She understood what the Marquis was implying and turned away to follow the *aide-de-camp*.

The Englishman opened the door on their left and announced the Marquis's name.

The Marquis found it was the office of Mr. Edward Rogers, the British Consul, and he rose from his desk and held out his hand.

"You wrote to me, my Lord, asking me to arrange a meeting for you with the Khedive yesterday morning," he began, "and I am so glad you have had time to visit me. If you remember, we met some years ago at a reception given by Lord Palmerston when he was Prime Minister."

"Of course we did. Your name was familiar, but I could not remember where we had met."

Mr. Rogers laughed.

"Well, now you are here is there anything I can do for you, my Lord?

"As a matter of fact there is. I wish to be married immediately and I will be more than grateful if you could make your Chaplain and your Chapel available for me."

Mr. Rogers drew in his breath.

He was a good-looking man nearing forty and had worked hard to reach the position he now occupied.

But he thought that this was the most extraordinary request he had ever heard in his long diplomatic career.

With some self-control he enquired,

"Is there any special reason, if it does not sound too inquisitive, why your Lordship should wish to be married so hastily?"

The Marquis then sat down in an armchair by the fireplace.

"I will tell you exactly what has happened," he said, "but as I have no wish for all this to be known in England or anywhere else, I must ask you to treat my story as totally confidential."

"But, of course, my Lord," Mr. Rogers agreed.

At the same time he was, as the Marquis realised, exceedingly curious.

The Marquis told him briefly all that had happened.

How Delia had run away because her father was forcing her to marry the Comte, as he believed him to be, having no idea that in his native country he was the Vizier to the Khedive of Egypt.

"I had always heard that he lived a double life, my Lord, and I knew he spent more time in Paris than he spent here. Actually here in Egypt he has an appalling reputation especially where women are concerned."

The Marquis nodded.

"That is as I suspected. The only way I can make certain that Miss Durham is safe is by making her my wife. Then we must leave Cairo as quickly as possible."

The Marquis admitted later that he had the greatest admiration for the way in which Mr. Rogers put the wheels in motion.

He rang a hand bell and sent for the Chaplain, who fortunately was in the Palace.

With what the Marquis considered must be record speed, he arranged that the marriage ceremony could take place as soon as Delia was ready.

"I hope, my Lord," Mr. Rogers said as the Chaplain left them, "that you will allow me to be your Best Man."

"It is most kind of you and I assure you that if I did not think that the situation was critical, I would not put you to all this trouble."

Mr. Rogers paused before he added very seriously,

"I would not want you or Miss Durham to be upset in any way if news of your marriage does make diplomatic relations more difficult than they are already."

The Marquis knew he was referring to the fact that the French would do everything in their power to prevent the English acquiring any part in the Suez Canal.

He could only hope that by some unexpected stroke of good fortune that Mr. Disraeli would be able to obtain the shares he so wanted for Great Britain.

*

Meanwhile Delia had found Mrs. Rogers charming and very helpful.

When the *aide-de-camp* had introduced her and the two women were alone, Delia asked her tentatively,

"Will you help me, Mrs. Rogers? The Marquis is asking your husband if we can be married immediately. If you would be kind and lend me some hairpins, I would like to put up my hair."

Mrs. Rogers looked at her in surprise.

"You are to be married here?" she then exclaimed. "How very exciting! But surely you are very young?"

Delia laughed.

"I have had to pretend to be very young ever since I left England. But actually I am getting on for nineteen and it is so wonderful that the Marquis wants to marry me. In fact, I am finding it difficult to believe it is really true."

"If you are to be a bride and such a lovely one too, you must let my maid arrange your hair. She is very good at it and I think it would be more appropriate if you wore a wreath instead of a hat."

"That would be fantastic!" Delia exclaimed.

Mrs. Rogers was just as efficient as her husband.

She took Delia into her bedroom and sent for her maid who was French.

When it was explained what was required, the maid was only too eager to make Delia look more grown-up and she arranged her hair in a most becoming way and it made her look considerably older.

By the time the French maid had finished with the arrangement, a wreath of small white flowers was brought to the bedroom by another maid.

The French maid had arranged Delia's hair on top of her head to give her height and the wreath fitted round it perfectly.

"You must also have a bouquet," Mrs. Rogers said. "I have asked them to give it to your future husband who should put it into your hands before you enter the Chapel."

They had just finished fixing the wreath in place when a servant knocked on the door.

He informed the maid that His Excellency and his Lordship were waiting downstairs.

"I do hope that you will allow me to come to your wedding," Mrs. Rogers asked Delia.

"But of course you must. You have been so kind and I just cannot thank you enough for making me look so different from when I arrived."

Now Mrs. Rogers put just a touch of powder on her face.

"Your skin is perfect," she said, "but you must look

a happy bride and when you arrived here, I could see you had been crying."

"I am so happy, so very happy, that I feel as if I am jumping over the moon. I am so afraid it is not real and I will wake up and find myself back at home."

Even as she spoke she thought that, however angry her father might be at her running away, he would never be able to beat her again.

She also thought that the Marquis was so important that her father would, in fact, be delighted at her marriage.

They walked downstairs.

When the Marquis saw her coming into the sitting room, he thought that no man could have a more beautiful and exquisite bride.

He picked up the bouquet of white lilies which was lying on the table and placed it in her arms.

Just for a brief second their eyes met and there was no need for words.

"If you are ready, my Lord," Mr. Rogers came in, "let me show you the way."

He walked out of the room.

Delia, with her bouquet of lilies over her left arm, slipped her right hand into the Marquis's.

His fingers closed over hers and she knew that she had never been so happy in the whole of her life.

They had only to walk a little way to the Chapel, which was built at one side of the Palace.

The Chaplain was waiting for them.

The Marriage Service was said very simply and yet with such a sincerity that made Delia feel that their vows joined them together so that they would never be apart.

At the same time she prayed fervently to God that the Marquis would love her as she loved him –

And that he would never become bored with her.

When the Chaplain blessed them, she felt as if all the angels in Heaven were singing in unison overhead.

She was sure that her mother was near her and was glad that she had found a man as wonderful as the Marquis to be her husband.

When the marriage ceremony was over they walked back into the Palace and then much to Delia's surprise Mr. Rogers suggested,

"I think, my Lord, you should leave at once and the quicker you are away from Cairo the better."

"That is exactly what I was thinking," the Marquis agreed.

"Of course I would like to drink to your health and happiness," Mr. Rogers went on, "but I think it is more important that you should leave Egypt without any delay."

"You are quite right and it is what I wish to do."

Their chaise was at the door, but now the hood had been raised.

Delia saw that there were two soldiers in uniform and armed sitting beside the driver.

There was also an Army vehicle containing half-a-dozen more soldiers under the command of a Sergeant-Major.

"I can never thank you enough," the Marquis was saying to Mr. Rogers, "for all you have done for us. I only hope that you and your wife will visit us when you are next in England."

"We will be delighted to do so, my Lord."

Mrs. Rogers kissed Delia saying,

"You are the most beautiful bride I have ever seen, and I know that you will both be extremely happy."

"Thank you, thank you both, Mr. and Mrs. Rogers," Delia exclaimed, "for everything."

As she stepped into the carriage she saw that her hat had not been forgotten – it was on the seat opposite her.

The Marquis joined her in the chaise and as he sat down she slipped her hand into his.

He smiled at her.

The hood of the chaise only covered the back seat and it was possible for anyone seated in front to look back and see what they were doing, so the Marquis did not put his arm round her.

When they were out of the grounds of the Palace and moving swiftly through the streets, Delia spoke for the first time.

"Is our escort coming with us on the yacht?"

"As far as Alexandria and as soon as we sail from there we will be out of Egypt. It will then be impossible for the Vizier to intimidate us anymore."

"Do you think he will try to get hold of me?" Delia asked in a frightened voice.

She knew only too well how revengeful an Oriental could be – and how he would lose face, if only in his own eyes, if he was unable to win what had become a battle between him and the Marquis.

"There is no need to be afraid," the Marquis said calmly. "But just in case he tries to cause trouble, the Consul felt that we should have an armed escort on-board. So you have absolutely nothing to worry about."

His fingers tightened on hers as if to make her feel safe.

Delia felt that there were no words appropriate for this special moment.

When they reached *The Scimitar*, the Marquis and Delia were piped aboard.

The Captain was given orders that they were to set sail immediately and as fast as possible down the Nile back to Alexandria.

It was one hundred and twenty miles away, and the Marquis knew that they would not be there much before the next morning.

He instructed the Captain to look after their escort of soldiers as well as the Sergeant-Major.

Meanwhile Delia walked into the Saloon and then because she felt shy she went down to her own cabin.

She placed her bouquet on the bed and stood at the porthole looking out over the landscape on the other side of the river.

It was impossible for her to believe that she was now a married woman and her husband was the Marquis.

How could it all have happened so suddenly?

She had thought when she saw the Vizier that she was lost and it would be impossible for anyone to save her.

The door of the cabin opened and the Marquis came in.

She turned round at the porthole and stood gazing at him.

"How could you have been just so wonderful?" she asked somewhat incoherently. "I did not mean you to be so involved with me in such an embarrassing and awkward way."

The Marquis smiled.

"It was not awkward for me, my Delia, I have been fighting from the start against falling in love with you, but if you had been using your incredible *Third Eye* you would have known that every day and every hour that passed by I loved you more and more."

"How could I have possibly known? How could I have guessed? Of course I love you, but I was afraid that when you took me back to England, I would never see you again."

"How on earth could you have thought of anything so ridiculous, my darling Delia?"

The Marquis now walked slowly towards her as if he was in no hurry.

As he reached her he breathed,

"Do you realise I have not yet, my darling, kissed you, although I have been tempted to do so a thousand and one times."

Delia felt a strange and wonderful feeling swell up within her breast.

Yet it was impossible to find even one word with which to answer him.

Very slowly the Marquis put his arms round her.

"Do you really think I would have allowed anyone to take you away from me, my dearest love? I just knew by the time we had reached Gibraltar that I wanted you as I have never wanted anyone before. I swear I will kill any man, including that swine I knocked out this afternoon, if he tries to take you from me."

Then very gently, as he realised she was trembling against him, the Marquis's lips found hers.

*

Sometime later the Marquis and Delia were served dinner together in the Saloon, while *The Scimitar* steamed at top speed down the Nile towards Alexandria.

Delia was still rather tense, feeling that they were still not quite out of danger, and the Marquis tried to take her mind off her fears by informing her that he intended to fulfil his promise and take her straight to Greece.

After dinner was over the Marquis went first to say goodnight to the Military Escort and then to give them a generous gratuity in case they disembarked at Alexandria before he was up in the morning.

Next he went to see the Captain on the bridge to instruct him to put the escort ashore at Alexandria and then to immediately set sail for Greece.

"I hope that you all enjoyed the champagne I sent for you to drink the health of my bride and myself," the Marquis commented before he left the bridge.

"We enjoyed it enormously, my Lord, and I'd like to wish you and her Ladyship every possible happiness.

"Thank you, Captain. We are both very grateful for all you have done."

"If you'll allow me to say so, my Lord," added the Captain, "I think her Ladyship is the most beautiful lady I've ever seen and, what's more, no one's more charming or more grateful for all that's been done for her."

"What you are really saying," the Marquis smiled, "is that I am a very lucky man."

"I think there's no man in the whole world who'd not think that, my Lord!"

The Marquis laughed and went below.

He had already told Hutton that Delia would sleep in the Master cabin and that he would use her cabin as his dressing room.

Hutton had transferred everything over while they were having dinner.

Now the Marquis dismissed Hutton and undressed himself.

Putting on a long flowing robe over his nightclothes he walked very quietly into the Master cabin.

He was thinking it quite possible that Delia would be asleep.

She was in fact watching the door for him to come to her.

There was only a small light on the table beside the bed and the moonlight coming through the portholes made the cabin appear mysteriously luminous.

"I thought you would be asleep," the Marquis said in a deep voice.

"How could I sleep when I was waiting for you – "

He took off his robe and threw it on a chair.

Then he climbed into the bed beside her.

She moved into his arms and laid her head against his shoulder.

"Is this really happening?" she asked in a whisper.

"If you mean 'am I your husband' the answer is a definite 'yes', and as the Captain has just said to me, you are the most beautiful bride there has ever been. I shall be extremely jealous of any man who thinks so as well!"

Delia gave a little laugh.

"There is only one man in the world who matters to me and that is *you*, my magnificent Marquis."

"Are you sure, Delia?"

"I love you," Delia sighed, "but I never dreamt you would love me. I only knew that when I had to leave you, it would be like dying."

"You will never leave me, Delia, and when we die, you well know that we will be together in another life."

"Do you really believe it now? You were somewhat sceptical when I first talked about it."

"I believe everything you say and I will never again argue with you when you use your *Third Eye*."

She knew that he was recalling how nervous she had felt on their way to see the dreadful Vizier – or, as she then thought of him, the Comte.

Even to think of him made her shiver and move a little closer to the Marquis.

"Forget him," he insisted. "He will never interfere in our lives again. But I will always be grateful that it was through him that I found you, my precious one."

"Of course it was, and I would never have run away if I had not been so terrified of him."

"I will protect you and save you from being afraid of anyone again, my darling. I have the idea I shall have to spend my time keeping away other men who want to take you from me."

Delia laughed.

"I know that no one could be as marvellous as you. But I am worried if I keep saying so, you will grow bored with me."

The Marquis knew from the way she spoke that it was a very real fear and he thought he knew why.

"I have only been bored in the past, my dearest one, because I had not found you. But now that I have found you, there are a million things for us to do together and I cannot imagine anything more exciting than to be with you while we are doing them."

"Oh, my darling, darling Rex! That is exactly how I want you to feel and think. Because you are so clever and at the same time so magnificent, I feel you will always be a leader whom people will follow. That means there is so much you can do for England, as well as for us."

The Marquis felt that she was inspiring him.

He would no longer waste his time with beautiful women who had always disappointed him and instead he would help those who really needed help and in that way, as Delia was implying, he could help England.

He pulled her a little closer to him.

"This is my wedding night, and now I am going to think, not of what I will do in the future, but how much I love you and how much, my gloriously lovely wife, I have to teach you about love."

Delia made a murmur of happiness and he went on,

"I am so afraid of frightening you and then losing you."

"You would never lose me, my dearest Rex, and it would be just impossible for you to frighten me. I am only rather scared that you may become bored or find me stupid and unintelligent about love. As you are aware, I know so little about it."

The Marquis thought that nothing would be more enthralling than to teach someone as innocent and unspoilt as Delia and to make her aware of his love for her.

It was so totally different from the love he had had for any other woman.

At the same time he knew that he would have to be very gentle.

He wanted to make her feel, as he was feeling, the wonder and glory of love as well as the irresistible fire that was consuming him.

His lips then sought hers and he kissed her at first gently, then more passionately.

When he raised his head he realised that the breath was coming very quickly from between her lips and when he touched her body she quivered beneath his.

Then he knew that the ecstasy he was feeling which was more intense and in a thousand ways different from anything he had ever felt before, she was feeling too.

"I love you. God, how much I love you, Delia. My precious, my darling, we will be very happy because every time I touch you I feel that I am getting nearer and nearer to Heaven itself."

"When you kiss me," whispered Delia, "I feel I am flying up into the sky and I can touch the stars and they are all a part of you, my magnificent Marquis."

"That is what I want you to feel, my darling. Yet I find it difficult to put all my feelings into words. So, my precious brilliant little wife, you must realise it with your *Third Eye*."

Delia gave a little chuckle.

"My *Third Eye* is telling me that this is the most perfect and wonderful moment of my life – and that love is even greater and more fulfilling than anything I have ever known or – dreamed about."

The words came from her lips a little jerkily.

The Marquis knew it was because her feelings were impossible to describe.

It was exactly what he felt himself and again there were no words he could find to describe them.

He kissed Delia until they were both flying up into the sky towards Heaven itself.

Then as he made Delia his, the Gates of Paradise opened.

They were one soul, joined together by the Love of God for all Eternity and beyond into Infinity.